MIDWATCH

PRAISE FOR *MIDWATCH*

"*Midwatch* heralds the arrival of a bright, new voice in literature. Like those midwatch hours where truths, traumas, and nightmares come to haunt, Danback-McGhan's exquisite and unforgettable stories reveal the ways that women are made to pay for serving in the military. Heartbreaking, funny, and wise, Danback-McGhan's debut will linger beyond the midwatch hours."

> —IVELISSE RODRIGUEZ, author of PEN/Faulkner Award
> for Fiction finalist *Love War Stories*

"Jillian Danback-McGhan arrives with a great blend of literary swagger and artistic vision. The stories that make up *Midwatch* are beautiful, sad, tender and fierce; from the streets of DC to the Gulf of Aden, we meet young women in the Navy trailblazing, and sometimes hell raising, for country. What a bold, brilliant debut."

> —MATT GALLAGHER, author of *Daybreak, Empire City*,
> and *Youngblood.*

"A Billy Budd-esque tale of self-defense against shipboard politics and sexual predators. A pod of garrison wives smells blood in pre-deployment waters. A modern woman-at-arms manifests as her own, self-actualized god of violence. These are gut-churning sea stories, worthy of standing any gothic lit-lover's graveyard shift—and each gritty enough to fuel a full-steam-ahead workshop on leadership ethics and military life. Soldier or sailor, veteran or citizen: Read. This. Book."

> —RANDY BROWN, co-editor of *Why We Write: Craft Essays*
> *on Writing War*

"From a hospital-induced haze, to abuses of power, *Midwatch* reveals a culture that contemporary war-lit has barely touched, showcasing the unique ways Navy characters make meaning of the inexplicable. No war-lit collection is complete without this book!"

> —KATEY SCHULTZ, author of *Still Come Home* and *Flashes of War*

"*Midwatch* pulled me in like Charybdis and left me swirling in a wreckage of wartime traumas, women's lives, and family dramas stuck in generational loops. These finely drawn portraits of Navy life ground universal tales of feminist horror in settings that are alternately terrifying and believable. Jillian Danback-McGhan is a marvel, and this collection will shatter you and leave you craving her next release."

—DR. LIAM CORLEY, author of *Unwound: Poems of Enduring War*

"These are the sea stories we've been waiting for. More than the prose, more than the characters, more than the plots (all and each of which are, let's be clear, amazing), it's the compelling urgency, the necessity of reading and listening to and heeding the clarion call in each of these sharp, taut tales: beware the power of stories, behold the power of stories. More than twenty years of war have scarred our nation and our planet, and *Midwatch* demands that we not look away, that we not stuff up our ears, that we believe the women who've sacrificed when they tell us what it cost."

—TRAVIS KLEMPAN, author of *Have Snakes, Need Birds* and *Hills Hide Mountains*

MIDWATCH

STORIES

JILLIAN DANBACK-MCGHAN

Published by Split/Lip Press
PO Box 27656
Ralston, NE 68127
www.splitlippress.com

ISBN: 978-1-952897-35-1

Cover and Book Design: David Wojciechowski
Editing: Pedro Ramírez

TABLE OF CONTENTS

INTRODUCTION

Midwatch was born from notes I scribbled in margins of notebooks I carried with me during my time as Surface Warfare Officer in the U.S. Navy. These notebooks accompanied me during deployments around South America, the Horn of Africa, and the Middle East; in classrooms at the United States Naval Academy; throughout the passageways of innumerable Washington, D.C. office buildings. I relegated the stories and characters created in these notebooks to the sidelines of the page, devaluing their merit even in my own mind, an internalization of what I saw occurring both in the military and in literature.

Women have fought in and written about every major war involving the United States since the American Revolution, yet this fact is frequently overlooked in the study of history and literature alike. Many brilliant writers and scholars have drawn attention to this oversight, particularly those who have written about women's involvement in the wars in Afghanistan and Iraq. Still, book-length fiction featuring women service members remains underrepresented in the cannon of military literature. Our efforts continue to be relegated to the midwatch, the period of time between evening and early morning spent entirely in darkness.

But the watch is changing. The promise of a sunrise wavers over the horizon. Reveille will be sounded soon. Until then, it is my sincere hope *Midwatch* will contribute to our foremothers' rich tradition of military writing and encourage other women servicemembers to bring their own stories into the light.

MIDWATCH

You know Ashleigh, right? She appeared everywhere a few years ago—newspapers, talk shows, they even had a congressional hearing about what happened. Every source had a spin. You could tell by the picture of Ashleigh they'd use. Picture one featured Ashleigh's boot camp photo, a typical smiling white girl, blonde hair slicked back in a tight bun. Her huge tits hidden under her blues, which made her look slightly chunky. Then there's picture two, an old modeling shot from back before Ashleigh joined the Navy. There she sits, this bleached-blonde sweetheart smiling in a camouflage-print bikini without much fabric to it. You can make out the tattoo on the inside of her left arm, the words *Noli me tangere* written in narrow, purple cursive. She gave the camera this sort of come-hither look, legs parted, a Remington Sendero in one hand, a deer carcass in another. Big buck, too. Ten points or more.

I grew up hunting. A kill is never that clean. There's no way Ashleigh got that buck herself.

The case, as most people knew it, goes like this: one morning, while the amphibious warship USS Mantis operated off the California coast for routine exercises, Lieutenant Anson Hart didn't show up for his divisional muster. The ship's crew checked his workspaces, paged him over the ship's 1MC. No luck. The crew feared the worst—three *Mantis* Sailors had jumped over the side the prior year. But his roommate swore that wasn't Hart. No, he claimed, that guy loved himself, a little too much. Still, Hart vanished. While the ship's master-at-arms searched his stateroom, the IT department searched his email and hard drive.

Everyone looked for a note. They found multiple notes instead. Declarations of love, warnings against infidelity. Threats to tell his boss about their relationship if he ever left her. All signed with Ashleigh's name in purple ink. In her locker, investigators found a Gerber knife with smudges of blood on the blade. They'd find traces of blood on Ashleigh's clothes later. They never found Hart's body.

I got assigned to *Mantis* fresh out of boot camp, about two months before the murder. The worst months of my life. Imagine—hundreds of people onboard, each running in their own direction with far less oversight than you'd expect from the military. See, the crew recently returned from an eight-month deployment and learned, a week after they pulled into homeport, they were set to head out on another deployment four months later. News of the tight turnaround left everyone onboard resigned and bitter; the crew moved without urgency, spoke without inflection, and answered innocent inquiries with a sneer. I expected a different experience when I graduated from boot camp. That I'd gain a sense of order in my life, perhaps. A way to see what I was capable of. Or maybe I'd simply find someone who gave a shit. That's what all the instructors promised, but I should've known better. Most promises are empty. No. This was the wilderness. I was left to fend for myself.

They dumped me in Deck Division with other new recruits, where I scrubbed decks and shined brass and greased bearings all day. I was supposed to get a running mate from my division when I arrived. Someone to help you adjust to ship life. You've probably guessed it by now: I got Ashleigh.

She waited for me on the quarterdeck when I first reported onboard. You couldn't miss her. She piled her bright blonde hair in a smooth bun atop her head. The thick layer of makeup she wore gave her skin a shiny, plastic look. She smiled and scowled at other crew members as they passed her by, laughing flirtatiously and giving them the finger in equal measure. Suffocating floral scents trailed behind her.

"Don't you have anything better to do then block my quarterdeck?" a chief asked Ashleigh as she stood there.

"Just waiting for you to notice me, chief," she said. In her TV interviews, Ashleigh had a meek, flirty Southern accent. She used this voice with the chief. Her words radiated from her chest, which she thrust in his direction.

"Take your trouble elsewhere," the chief replied.

"Relax, chief. I'm playing with you. We've got a new girl coming today. Gonna show her around. You know how serious I am about my work."

"What kind of work is that, exactly?" asked a petty officer lurking behind her.

"None of your goddamn business," she responded, changing her voice to a nasal whine. A tone so sharp she could've stabbed this guy through the heart with it.

The petty officer lifted his hands and backed away.

"You the new girl?" She asked. I nodded.

"Then quit your staring," she said and threw the bundle she held at her side at me. Later, I'd inspect the contents and find a laundry bag, some sheets, a pair of work gloves, and a Gerber multi-tool stuffed inside.

"We muster at seven," she said. "I'm supposed to be your running mate, but my time don't come cheap. I'll expect you to do my laundry for it."

I smirked, thinking this was her way of testing me. Her sour expression suggested otherwise.

"I can find my own way around," I said, lifting my chin a little.

"Well, well," she replied. "Let's see how you do."

I entered the skin of the ship, heavy seabag shifting on my back, the awkward bundle Ashleigh gave me dangling at my side. Crew members rushed through the passageway as a single swell of blue-clad bodies, shutting the solid watertight doors behind them. Heavy thuds and metallic squeals. An alarm sounded over the ship's 1MC.

"Get to your station!" someone yelled as he ran past.

"Move!" said another.

"What's happening?" I asked a senior chief who happened to be rushing by.

"We're in the middle of a drill. Where do you belong?" he asked.

"I just got here," I said.

"Then get down to the mess decks."

"Where's that, Senior?"

"Figure it out," he said, pointing at the steady flow of Sailors who traveled toward the same destination.

The mess decks looked like any cafeteria might—long lines of benches, a buffet counter, blue vinyl upholstered tables. Except the drill activities transformed it into a triage center. Sailors laid out heavy oxygen tanks, masks, and hoses on the blue upholstered tabletops. They donned heavy boots and helmets, tucked their pant legs into their socks and rushed in and out of the space in response to commands called over the 1MC.

"You there," a first class petty officer pointed at me as I huddled in a corner. He handed me a laminated card with the words *abdominal wound* printed on it. "Make yourself useful."

He hoisted me onto a table and directed three other Sailors to administer to my fictitious wounds. They hastily prodded my torso. I found a bruise on my ribcage the next day.

"What do we check for first?" the first-class asked.

"The same thing we always look for," a third-class petty officer replied.

"How many times are we going to do this damn drill?" asked another.

"Twice a week until deployment," the first-class responded. "More if the XO catches you messing around, so focus."

"Could someone show me where female berthing is located when this is done?" I asked. The other petty officers hovered over me like vultures over carrion.

"Forward or aft?" one of the Sailors asked.

"Stop talking. You're near death," the first-class said.

I imagined what my injury looked like. Was it a neat, hollow perforation, like a direct shot to the torso? Or a jagged wound where the skin unevenly tears, the kind animals get from jagged branches when fleeing a predator?

One of the hovering Sailors, a third-class, bent close and whispered into my ear.

"You can follow me down there when the drill is done," she said. "But don't walk too close. And don't tell Ashleigh I helped you."

"Why not?" I asked.

"No pulse," the third-class yelled, and laid another card on my chest: *dead.*

There were no empty racks in berthing, so I spent the night on the grimy floor, curled around my sea bag and tucking my arms inside my coveralls for warmth. I woke up with a cramp in my side. My skin no longer smelled of the brackish brook water and woodsmoke odors from home, but of exhaust and sweat and stale air. Ashleigh stood over me as I laid there.

"How'd your first day go?" she asked and dropped her laundry bag at my feet. I picked it up and let Ashleigh lead me to my rack, one directly underneath hers. She kicked me every time she got in and out of it.

This all sounds pathetic, I know. Back then, I felt I had no other choice. I knew nothing about this strange world I joined and was too timid to speak out about it. The other girls onboard confirmed my fears when they cautioned me to stay quiet. It wasn't worth the trouble, they said, because of the Lieutenant.

You see, Ashleigh had been with our division officer, Lieutenant Hart, for over a year. All the enlisted knew, but no one would report them. It'd probably get brushed off as enlisted gossip, anyway. Why invite trouble by snitching?

Like all good predators, Hart's appearance concealed him. He had gangly limbs and a protruding Adam's apple, a hooked nose, ears fanning out from his head like antlers. Yet unlike other officers, who never stopped running their mouths, Hart rarely spoke. He maintained eye contact for far too long and would gaze at you with this deep, unrelenting stare. The kind of look that made you feel trapped.

"And who is this?" Hart asked as he surveyed me on the morning of my first divisional muster. He stood close enough for me to smell scrambled eggs lingering on his breath and synthetic vanilla fumes from his aftershave.

"The new girl. I'm showing her around," said Ashleigh, who stood to my right.

"God help her," someone in the formation said.

Everyone laughed.

"Shut it. Think I'm worried about ugly thing?" She replied.

Everyone laughed again.

"Lock it up," Hart said. Then, giving me a wink, added, "Our new recruit is in exceptional hands."

From the corner of my eye, I caught Ashleigh scowling at me.

"Damn, girl," the guy standing on my left whispered. "I'd watch out if I were you."

Hart read off our assignments for the day and tasked Ashleigh to verify they were completed. As he spoke, he fixed his gaze on me without looking away. It made me want to scamper off and burrow a hole into the deck like some meek woodland creature. He dismissed us and the division scattered, each person setting off to their work. I felt a solid kick to the back of my knees as I walked away and hit the deck hard, my chin catching the rough surface first. All my breath left my chest.

"Walk much, newbie?" Ashleigh asked, giggling as she stepped over me and left the compartment. No one offered to help me up.

I thought about home as I laid there. The backwoods of Pennsylvania. Real wilderness. It felt like I never left. Which seemed too cruel, considering I joined the Navy to get out of the goddamn wilderness.

*

After high school, I wound up cleaning rooms in one of those couples' resorts in the Poconos, pulling globs of semen-soaked hair from shower drains. Vacuuming fake velvet curtains and changing shit-stained sheets on heart-shaped beds. My stepbrothers would joke about me becoming one of the hotel night workers, an allusion I didn't get until a few weeks in, when I realized I saw the same women—easily recognizable by their sallow faces and thick eyeliner—prowling around one of the hotel's side doors. Each night, they'd lead a different greasy man back to their rooms. Each morning, I'd hope to find one of their clients sprawled across the heart-shaped bed, stabbed or strangled to death. Each day, I went about my work disappointed.

Hunting provided my only respite. I loved being out in a deer blind on my own, attuned to every snapping twig or rustling leaf. The one place my inconspicuousness served me well. I spent most of my waking hours being overlooked and disregarded, but hiding is your greatest advantage when you're out in the woods. It gives you control. Even on the days when it poured and my fingers numbed, I could remain in the woods for hours, fetid with the scent of deer piss, content as twilight dissolved the trees to gnarled, blackened shapes.

Most importantly, hunting kept me away from my asshole father and idiot stepbrothers who'd drink themselves stupid with their buddies and pass out in the yard nightly. Every so often, Bucky, one of their friends, would find his way into my part of the trailer and climb into bed with me.

"I've heard stories about you, you know," he'd whisper. "Come on."

I would lay perfectly still and shut my eyes, hoping it would deter his groping. Frantically thinking how I could escape without waking my father, who'd only fling me across the room and call me foul names. If I ran into him in the daytime, Bucky would blow me a kiss and raise his eyebrows whenever my stepbrothers weren't looking.

Bucky didn't stop one night. Didn't roll off me with an exasperated sigh and storm out when I refused to move. He peeled away my sweatpants, fumbled with the button of his own jeans. Snorted and wheezed the entire time, like a deer in rut. Without thinking, I lunged for the rock I kept on my nightstand, a heavy chunk of quartzite I found when playing in the woods as a kid.

Bucky's hands were too far up my shirt to react to the first strike. He looked too confused to react to the second. He staggered out of my room, stunned, and collapsed on the ground outside of our trailer. My stepbrothers hooted at this display, probably thinking he got sloppy drunk. They tossed him in the back of his truck to sleep it off, too high to notice the blood welling at his temple.

When I finished work the next day, I stopped by a recruiter's office to enlist. Took the first billet the recruiter offered. He didn't ask for details or question the bruising on my left hand. To avoid facing Bucky again, I slept in empty hotel rooms at the resort until my date to report to Great Lakes arrived. I brought the rock with me and left it on the sink when I disembarked at O'Hare. I like to think it's still there, a gray marbled stone spattered with dark red, an oddity overlooked by passengers washing their hands and fixing their hair before going to their next destination.

*

Midwatch is a time for storytelling. It's the watch between ten at night and two in the morning, that span of nothingness between the late evening and early morning. Topside lookouts like to tell tales to keep themselves awake, the more outrageous the better. It's a long-standing tradition. The job would be boring otherwise. All you do is stand at fixed locations on the ship's deck and report anything you see, like other ships, marine life, people trying to jump overboard. It reminded me of being in the deer blinds. You can see everything around you, yet no one notices you lurking in the dark. We were supposed to rotate watches, but I always traded to get the midwatch. I craved the solitude of the ship at night. Through these disembodied voices running through the communications network in our headsets, I obtained most of my information on Ashleigh and Lieutenant Hart.

"I heard Hart and Ashleigh are playing their game again," a lookout said one evening.

"What game?" I asked.

"Oh, Hart sleeps around for fun," another lookout said. "He loves messing with enlisted girls. Especially the real young ones."

"Didn't he get one pregnant?"

"Eh, she got around. No one knows the real father."

"Wait, I thought she claimed she was pregnant, but wasn't?"

"But aren't he and Ashleigh a thing?" I asked. The other lookouts laughed.

"He likes making her jealous. She loses her mind when she catches him cheating."

"Respect for that dude. He pulls it in for having such a broke face."

"And Ashleigh marks her territory. Tossed another girl's stuff overboard when we were out to sea a few months ago. Everything in her locker. Wallet, laptop, keys. Everything."

"Two of Hart's former girls jumped overboard," one lookout said. "The ship pulled one out of the water, but it was too late by then."

"Naw, both were batshit. Don't think Hart had anything to do with either."

"I was on watch when the second one jumped. Called it in myself."

"Man, all your bullshit stories. You say you were on watch for everything."

"No, it's true!"

"How has no one done anything?" I asked.

"Won't change anything. Who's going to believe some enlisted over an officer?"

"Besides, I hear his dad is some important admiral or something."

"I heard Captain?"

"Whatever. It doesn't matter. All the officers and chiefs are too busy doing their own thing to care. Especially with this bullshit deployment coming up."

"You're in deck division, aren'tcha? I'd keep my distance."

"What does she have to worry about? No offense, girl."

"Naw, he'll go for it. Y'all knows Hart sticks it in whatever moves."

I had already started to worry. It was nothing at first. A look from Hart that lasted a bit too long, even for him. A few times when he put his hands on my waist as he tried to pass by me in a narrow space.

"Easy on the chow line," he'd say. "You're starting to fill out."

Then I suddenly found myself assigned to tasks alone. I'd be told to scrub and sweep infrequently traveled parts of the ship, to replace lights in the helicopter tower, or check for rust in the anchor windless. Hart would inevitably appear to show me what I was doing wrong by putting his hand on mine or leaning across my body with his. To give me some instruction, as he put it. I'd thank him for his help and move away as quickly as I could. He'd laugh at my anxious movements. Tell me what a good job I was doing.

One night, as I worked in a storeroom adjacent to some noisy engineering equipment, I felt him press his body against mine. The hum of the machinery muffled his approach. He'd looped his arm around my waist before I could react.

"You know, I've seen the way you look at me," he said. "We should talk about this."

A high-pitched ringing filled my ears. My body tensed and no longer obeyed the commands I gave it, as if it were no longer my own.

"Aren't you quiet?" he said. Then, whispering in my ear, he added, "Think about it. I'm not going anywhere."

I collapsed into a ball when he left. Too stunned to move. Not caring who found me. Hart's advances or Ashleigh's retaliation—what I feared more, I couldn't say. Ashleigh appeared at the entrance to the storeroom a few minutes later.

"What do you think you're doing?" Ashleigh asked. "This was supposed to be done by now."

I jumped to my feet.

"Then send someone to help," I said. "It's too much for one person."

"Keep bitching and you'll end up with more," Ashleigh said. "Speaking of which, I'm running low on t-shirts."

"Self-service laundry is always packed," I said. "I can do it back in port."

"Or you can do it when you're done with the midwatch," she said with a grin. "Since you love standing it for some weird-ass reason. I hear no one's down there at three in the morning."

Back in bootcamp, our drill instructors told us that any problems should be brought to our divisional chiefs. It was their job to help. The problem was, I'd only seen our divisional chief once. Everyone on *Mantis* called him Chief Jabba and he remained in the Chiefs Mess doing paperwork most days. The other lookouts said the gout in his foot prevented him from wandering the deck plates, but his impairment wasn't bad enough for the Navy to send him to a shore command for limited duty.

A chief I didn't recognize answered the door to the Chiefs Mess.

"What do you want?" He asked. "They're setting up for lunch."

"I'm looking for Chief Ja- um, Chief Brenner?"

"You shouldn't be doing business in the Mess," the chief said. The chiefs onboard regarded the Mess as hallowed ground, their personal respite from whiny Sailors and demanding officers. Behind him, I could see the dull glow of brass plaques, five-inch shells, framed news articles, and gilded lanyards covering the bulkheads. Artifacts they collected to lend credibility to the stories they told of *Mantis*'s past victories.

"I know, Chief," I said. My voice wavered and my throat felt dry. "Couldn't find him anywhere else."

"That tracks," the chief said. "C'mon in."

Chief Jabba pouted as I entered the Mess. "You're the one who joined last month," he said. "What's the problem?"

His bootless foot rested a chair with a wilting ice pack draped on top. His pinkie toe, swollen to the size of a cucumber, peeked out of a hole in the side of his sock.

"It's just, things aren't what I thought they'd be," I replied.

Chief Jabba laughed. "Did you expect a Caribbean cruise?"

"It's Lieutenant Hart," I said. "He, um, leads the division in a way that's, um...strange."

"I don't have all day."

"He put Ashleigh in charge of checking work. She's only a second class."

"Yeah, she's a fast one," Chief said, whistling between his teeth. "But she gets things done. And she's here. Know how many in Deck we've lost this year?"

"No."

"Nine. Five to injury, plus four others who got picked up for augmentations with the Army. Three in Afghanistan, one in Iraq. And it's not just Deck. A third of our crew is out on augmentations. The last first-class we had in Deck was kicked out for a DUI; the one before him popped positive on our last drug test. The one we have now is too goddamn stupid to tie his own boots."

He adjusted his fleshy frame from the chair, groaning as he moved. "My point is, Lieutenant's got a squad full of turds. Sometimes, you gotta go with the least runny one. Understood?"

"Yes, Chief. I do. It's just that Lieutenant Hart looks at me this weird way. And the way he says things. I don't know how to describe it."

"Let me get this straight. You're here to tell me a story 'bout a second-class stepping up and your division officer looking at you funny?"

I looked down at the speckled deck beneath my boots. It did sound absurd.

"She makes me do her laundry."

"Yeah, she does that," Chief chuckled. "This your first time away from home?"

I nodded.

Chief flexed his puffy foot, causing the ice pack resting on top to plop onto the deck. He strained to grab it, impeded by the mound of his own gut. I picked it up and handed it to him. A small stream of water trickled from the corner of the ice pack.

"You seem like a good kid," he said. "But this crew's been shafted real hard. If the Lieutenant looks at you funny, look away. He's probably got other things on his mind. You can do well here, but you gotta get with the program. Understood?"

"Understood, Chief."

"Good. Now get out. Lunch is coming. It's taco day."

*

Later that night, I dreamed about the sallow-faced women at the hotel back at home.

*

Two weeks later, *Mantis* was out for our final round of at-sea exercises before deployment. While conducting inventory in the boatswain's locker, Hart entered the compartment and shut the hatch behind him.

"It's time we had our conversation," he said as he pressed himself against me. "We'll leave for deployment soon. We should get this thing between us resolved before then."

"I have to finish up, sir," I stuttered. "I have the midwatch."

"Come on," he said. "I've seen so many girls like you. You act all innocent for a while, then you strike. Let's not play games, OK?"

I tried to step away, but he wrapped his arms around my waist and pulled me back. I froze, frantic as a trapped doe.

"Not now," I whispered. "I'll be late. Meet me topside at one." His damp breath quickened against my neck. He departed without another word.

For the first three hours of my watch, I slouched against the ship's hull, moving only to remove a section of the ship's lifelines near my post. An escape if I needed it. The other lookouts chatted away, but I remained silent except to give the "All conditions normal" report at the top of each hour. The new moon cast no light on the water's surface. Mars flickered its red light. The motion of the ship made it look as if the Pleiades gave Orion chase.

Hart's silhouette emerged topside right on time. Men are always punctual when sex is involved.

"Clever of you," he whispered and looked around at the empty deck, absent of any illumination except for the thin sliver of a waning moon. "All anyone will see are two shadows."

He caressed the zipper at the top of my coveralls, then yanked it down to my waist. He pressed his mouth into mine so hard that my jaw ached.

"Wait," I said, turning my head so I could breathe.

For a moment, things didn't seem so bad. I could get with the program, like Chief said. Do Ashleigh's bidding. Keep still until Hart loses interest, just like those nights back at home. That is, until Hart emitted a disturbing groan. A guttural sound. Just like an animal.

I struck. He stopped.

Hart didn't stagger backwards until I stabbed him in the side a second time, twisting the blade and dragging it toward the center of his stomach. To stab into flesh isn't an easy feat, you see. It helps to thrust twice, once to break through the soft tissue and a second time to really do some damage.

He clutched at his stomach with one hand and raised his other arm to block any additional strikes I might deliver. I had no intention of making contact. He continued moving backwards without noticing the missing life-lines. He disappeared over the side and sunk under the foamy wake the ship's hull sliced into the black water below.

The scent of rust overwhelmed the salty air. I stood for a minute, then two, as if to wake myself from a dream. The sound of a hatch slamming from across the deck shook me out of it. I put on my work gloves to replace the lifelines, then hunched back against the hull of the ship, counting the ocean swells to calm my breathing. I meant to toss the Gerber overboard, but somehow this detail slipped my mind until my watch relief tapped me on the shoulder. The blood on my hands had congealed to a sticky paste, so I made it to the showers without leaving a trail. After washing the blood from my hands and wrists, I tucked my coveralls and gloves in the laundry bag Ashleigh left on my rack and proceeded to the laundry room.

The laundry spun. My mind churned. The swirl of the washer measured the meter of my thoughts. I did what I had to do. All I needed to do was put the laundry away. Return topside. Throw the knife overboard.

Reveille hadn't been sounded yet when I returned to berthing. No one stirred. A few girls snored. I tiptoed through the space, careful not to wake anyone. As I hung Ashleigh's laundry bag on the hook at the front of her locker, she threw back her blackout curtains and sprung from her rack. I leapt backwards and gasped.

"Dramatic much," she said, her voice hoarse upon waking. She pointed at the laundry bag. "You didn't fold it."

Ashleigh opened her locker and stripped in front of me, letting her mesh shorts and t-shirt drop to the floor. She pulled on a spotted, tan-colored terrycloth robe and shuffled off to the shower, an incarnadine towel draped languidly over her arm. Watching her overwhelmed me with a violent hunger. Her robe looked like animal skin, her towel a strip of exposed flesh. Despite my racing heart, I slowed my breathing more out of instinct than thought. My muscles tensed with anticipation—the sinewy recoil proceeding a pounce.

I never returned topside to dispose of the knife. I proceeded to the sink instead and rinsed the Gerber's handle, but not the blade, wrapping it in a towel to avoid touching it. Then I returned to Ashleigh's locker, used my sleeve to open the latch, and placed the Gerber inside.

*

The woman at Ashleigh's trial had no resemblance to the girl I knew onboard *Mantis*. In courtroom photos, she appeared much thinner than I remembered and she had dyed her hair a flat mousy brown. Ashleigh's face, absent of any make-up, looked slack and wan. She claimed Hart had coerced her into sleeping with him, just like the others. She even described a conversation with Jabba similar to mine. The difference, Ashleigh claimed, is that she had used this to her advantage.

"I didn't kill Anson," she sobbed when she took the stand. "Why would I? He gave me the little power I had on that ship. Why would I kill him if I got so much from being with him? Yes, I abused this position sometimes. People say I was a bully, and maybe I was. What other choice did I have? You either got knocked over or were the one who did the shoving."

How much of this image her lawyers cultivated for the trial is anyone's guess. The hollow expression she wore, though, couldn't be faked. Her eyes seemed devoid of all nervousness and hope. Most of all, Ashleigh looked empty—a blank space waiting to be written upon. All predators have their means of survival. I had misunderstood hers.

The prosecution did their best to depict Ashleigh as the predator and to gloss over Hart's indiscretions. Why wouldn't they? Animals so beautiful and brazen can't be anything but deadly. No testimony could ever turn over Ashleigh's conviction. This frees and ensnares me: on those rare nights, when complacent safety makes me forget my instincts for survival and my chest constricts with guilt, I'm reminded I'll never be able to confess. People will always see me as one of those lunatics who attach themselves to tragedy. The story is set. I don't fit within it.

A few members of the crew testified at the trial. They acknowledged hearing rumors about Hart but didn't believe any of it; the son of a famous admiral would always attract nasty gossip. Except the famous admiral and his elegant wife weren't sitting in the front row of the gallery. A leather-skinned Orlando police officer and a middle school teacher in a poorly fitted black suit sat there instead, staring into the middle distance with red-rimmed eyes. Turns out Hart had the same name as the famous admiral but bore no relation to him. Everyone believed the wrong story.

*

After Hart went missing, Mantis returned to port and the Coast Guard took over the search for his body. Investigators came onboard to detain Ashleigh and interviewed everyone in Deck division, including me. I said I knew nothing. I'd heard stories about Hart and Ashleigh, sure, but who knew what to believe. One of the investigators asked me why no one said anything.

"Nobody would listen," I said.

This was a lie. All anyone ever did was listen. Night after night, we listened to the same tired plot lines, the same characters, the same predictable endings. We frightened ourselves into submission by listening to tales which set the parameters for what we thought was possible. No one questioned whether these stories were true. No one wondered whether they held us back.

I guess I got tired of hearing the same story over and over. I wanted a different type of story. I wanted another kind of ending.

HAIL AND FAREWELL

"Grant is cheating on Emiko," Bethany said, instantly attracting the attention of all the women assembled in Sara Brant's kitchen for the weekly Wardroom Wives Wine Night. Bethany possessed a high-pitched voice which made Sara's ears ache. "I overheard Demetri last night. He was talking to someone on the phone, don't know who, and I heard him say how he walked in on Grant messing around with the new officer onboard. Then he says, 'Shitty thing to do because he's married, but whatever man, I'm staying out of it.' I tried to ask him about it later, but he just said it was nothing."

"Poor Emiko," Celia said. "Such a meek little thing. I heard Grant married her when he was stationed in Japan. These men who go and marry the local girls without even speaking their language. They should be ashamed of themselves."

"Doesn't Grant speak Japanese, though?" asked Monica, the chief engineer's wife. "He and I talked about it once. You know, I studied in Japan for my graduate degree." The other women ignored Monica. She mentioned she had her master's in every conversation, a habit they all found highly annoying. As if they all didn't abandon some portion of themselves when they got married.

"I heard the girl involved is a real slut," Bethany said. "Nicola's her name. One of Demetri's friends from ROTC knew a guy who used to date her college roommate."

"Nicola Mattingly," Celia chimed in. "Bruce said she's one of the three new officers onboard. The only woman, so she must be the one."

"I saw her a few days ago when I brought Ed his dinner on the ship. She's cute in the way all girls are when they're, what, twenty-three?" said another woman.

"Ugh, I don't think so. Those girls look so mannish," said another.

"Poor Emiko. Bad enough your husband's messing around. Worse when she's ugly," another chimed in.

Sara set down the horseshoe-shaped cheese tray she had been carrying. Her hands shook too furiously to carry the object any further. Listening to her guests bray about their Nicola-sightings and Grant's infidelities made Sara recall the time she discovered her own mother, puffy-eyed and ragged, sitting in the corner of her bedroom closet, half-hidden behind a row of long evening gowns dangling from their hangers.

"Ladies! Let's not lose sight of the main issue here," Sara said. All eyes in the room darted from Bethany to Sara. Bethany pouted. "Grant may be a dog, but there's a deployment on the horizon and a precedent to be set. Our husbands are already under enough pressure without tossing a bunch of shameless young girls into the mix." Sara paused for effect, continuing only when she heard her guests' soft murmurs of concern.

"You hear things, sure, and think that this could never happen to us. I remember the stories my mother would tell. Believe me, it can happen to any one of us."

The women looked down, swirling the wine in their glasses. They cherished the lives they lived, for the most part—steady employment for their husbands, frequent parties and annual balls, the prestige the profession attracted. They also felt throbbing reminders of what they gave up. The jobs they didn't get due to gaps on their resumes. The deaths of parents they missed while their husbands were stationed overseas. The months they spent sleeping alone in rented houses in unfamiliar neighborhoods. They could defend these decisions for love or duty; to have infidelity as your reward seemed unfathomably cruel.

"I'll talk to Bruce about it," Celia said. "He'll put a stop to this behavior."

As the commanding officer's wife, she was supposed to be their leader. Though the other women tolerated Celia's presence more than they respected it. Celia moved anxiously and hastily, and possessed a round, doughy face which Sara always wanted to slap.

Rank is not pedigree, Sara's mother used to say.

"Good idea, Celia," Sara said, forcing a smile. "Perhaps we should send a message of our own? Bruce has enough to worry about. And Emiko will suffer if her husband's career does."

"Like what?" Bethany asked with a note of annoyance in her voice. Sara smiled.

"Celia will be hosting all of us at her house for a Hail and Farewell next week for all the new wardroom members and those that are departing," Sara said. "This Nicola girl is new, no? We must celebrate her arrival."

*

Whenever Sara thought of her mother, she envisioned her with a place card in her hand. Like a tarot card reader who attended finishing school, Renee Carlson divined her family's destiny with these 3x2 inch pieces of stationery.

"Parties are hard work," she explained when Sara was ten years old and asked to attend soccer tryouts at her new elementary school instead of helping her mother prepare for a party.

"These are events designed to promote your father's career. He supports us, so it is our job to support him. Besides," Renee paused to rearrange silverware on their dining room table. "Soccer doesn't sound very ladylike."

Instead of after school activities, Sara assisted her mother with party planning. When she didn't help her mother at their house, Sara's mother lent her out to other wardroom wives for their parties and events. Of course, Renee's expected a full report when Sara returned home: *What did the inside of Admiral Bannon's house look like? Did Captain Vicars behave himself? I heard he has a wandering eye.*

Sara, for her part, didn't mind it, especially when it meant she could create floral arrangements while her brother toiled over math homework upstairs. She moved with her family too often to become a curious student and never adjusted to the different curricula offered in each new state. Besides, parties thrilled her. Sara loved to watch guests surge through a house, bringing it to life with their peals of laughter, the din of ice rattling in glasses, overlapping conversations, abstract images created by wine stains on cocktail napkins.

Sara's love of parties seemed inevitable, as she assumed all of Renee's interests and aligned her aspirations wherever her mother directed them. Who else could she emulate? Her father, defined more by his prolonged absences than any other attribute? Her brother, who spent his time being shuffled off to water polo and SAT tutorials? It seemed as if nature itself ordained Sara to become an extension of her mother. They shared the same honey-blonde hair and piercing blue eyes, identical round faces with undefined cheekbones, and similar (if somewhat unfortunate) short, squat builds.

"An inheritance from our ancestors," Renee would say whenever Sara bemoaned her figure. "We can thank the Cavaliers for gravitas and a lack of height. Good breeding has its occasional downfalls."

When she hosted parties at the Carlson residence, Renee would mention her esteemed lineage when giving guests a tour of their house. A prominent feature of her parents' house, wherever they moved, included an oil painting of a flamboyantly dressed man with old-fashioned britches and puffy sleeves, sandy-colored hair, and a broad hat topped with a feather.

"That's one of my forefathers, a renowned English Cavalier and former equerry to King Charles," Renee would tell guests as she took them from room to room. "He came to the States and founded the Jamestown colony. Jamestown families are older than those boastful Mayflower folks, you know. Our family heirlooms are older than this country." Renee neglected to mention how this particular family heirloom was a replica.

Sara was fifteen when she found her mother hiding in her closet, sobbing over her father's latest infidelity. She had long suspected her parents weren't happy. They rarely spoke to each other, and when they did, their voices sounded clipped and business-like. She couldn't remember her parents showing any affection towards each other aside from ship homecomings, when returning officers were expected to greet their wives on the pier with an embrace. Seeing her mother entirely devoid of composure terrified Sara. This had to be some imposter—she'd find the real Renee downstairs in the kitchen, with precise makeup and shiny hair, planning her menu for a party later this week.

"He's embarrassed me again," Renee said in a ragged voice. A line of mascara bled down her cheek. Renee made no attempt to wipe it away.

"Dad would never," Sara said. "You said he does everything for us."

"Oh, grow up," Renee responded. "All of this is for his own ego."

"Then why do you help him so much?" Sara asked.

Renee ignored her daughter's question. "The bastard left letters lying around, Sara. He doesn't even care. And with Commander Rinna's wife, no less! Word gets out about this, and his career is over. Where would we live then?"

Sara offered to get her mother something, an offer extended less from sympathy and more as a way to escape. Renee told Sara to head over to Mrs. Blake's house to avoid being late. Sara returned several hours later to find her mother sprawled in a pile of her shoes, her wedding band tinkling at the bottom of an empty vodka bottle. The letters Renee mentioned earlier were spread across the floor. Sara collected them and covered her mother with a coat dangling from its hanger.

She knew she shouldn't have read the letters. Still, she couldn't help herself, even though she knew the prurient details pertained to her own father, a man who wore tube socks with deck shoes and picked dried boogers with his pinkie when he thought no one was looking. How anyone could see him as an object of desire baffled Sara as much as it disgusted her. Mrs. Rinna spared no details, either. In addition to writing dirty notes to Sara's father, she included her opinions of other Navy wives, belittled her own husband, and even confessed the times she'd cheated on him in the past. Sara felt a burning sensation in her stomach and chest as she read each letter. She lay in bed contemplating ways to make this woman pay. By dawn, she had a solution.

Maribelle Osborne, wife of the commodore of Destroyer Squadron Twenty-two, had asked Sara to assist at a dinner she hosted for squadron commanding officers and their families. Commander Rinna would attend—he commanded the highest performing ship on the Mayport waterfront—and, from Sara's review of the guest list, Mrs. Rinna would join him.

Sara arrived at the party a few minutes late and made her apologies to Mrs. Osborne, explaining that she needed to make up some work at school, which was why she brought her backpack with her. Maribelle didn't mind. She felt reassured having such a nice girl like Sara available to lend a hand. Everyone knew Sara provided the magic touch when it came to the tiny details which made a party memorable. Could she start setting the table? She heard Sara made beautiful napkin origami. Sara agreed, and once Maribelle left the room, she removed several slips of paper from her backpack and folded each into the napkin fabric.

Renee always cautioned Sara against causing a scene: *public hysteria is the surest indicator of poor breeding*. Sara thought of her mother's maxim as she watched Mrs. Rinna read the note folded into her napkin. The woman stood so abruptly she knocked over a water glass and demanded to know where this note came from. At the same time, the rest of the guests read their own notes, and the party erupted with similar outbursts.

"I did not have my nose done!" Mrs. Blake shrieked.

"You slept with her?" Mrs. Harris asked, turning to her husband with wild eyes.

"This is your handwriting!" Commander Rinna said. "Christine, what did you do?"

The party devolved into chaos. Mrs. Harris dove toward Mrs. Rinna, but Mrs. Blake restrained her. Unable to reach Mrs. Rinna, Mrs. Harris grabbed a plate of shrimp and hurled it at Mrs. Rinna, hitting Commander Scott instead. Commander Rinna then tackled Commander Harris and the two men collapsed onto the floor, striking at one another on the way down. Captain Osborne bellowed for everyone to stop. The guests were too busy hollering and thrashing and shrimp-throwing to care.

After the initial outbreak of hostilities, Sara snuck out of the house through the back door. She skipped on her way home, fighting the urge to break out into a full-blown sprint (*Only thieves and children run*, Renee would say), but leaping into the air at different intervals, letting out cackles of glee. The nervousness plaguing her prior to the party deliquesced into pure, delicious elation.

This must be what power feels like, Sara thought. She always equated it with domineering men who wore large class rings and gave orders to move ships or men or families. She possessed a different kind of power—the unseen hand that shaped fate, just like her mother did with her place cards.

The next morning, as she got ready for school, Sara heard her mother chatting on the phone downstairs.

"She did what? Maribelle, I don't know what to say. Oh. Oh my, and he threw Christine out? I had no idea. Yes, I'll speak with her now. Thank you." Renee hung up the phone and shouted for Sara to come downstairs.

"What happened at Maribelle's last night?" Renee asked. "Her guests found notes tucked into their napkins at dinner?"

Sara looked down and didn't answer, so she did not see Renee approach and wrap her in the tightest embrace Sara had ever received. Renee kissed the top of Sara's head repeatedly, then pulled her into her chest again.

"I'm so proud of you," Renee whispered.

*

Three years later, when her father received an appointment to serve as the President of the Naval War College in Newport, Sara enrolled at a small college nearby so she could help her mother on weekends. Regardless, she and her mother had increasingly less to discuss. Sara studied business and talked about starting her own party-planning business when she graduated, a plan which Renee vehemently opposed.

"What makes you think you can succeed?" Renee would ask. "Aren't my parties important enough for you?" Her insistence that Sara return home for the summer instead of heading to Boston for an internship only heightened the tension between them.

Sara knew the source of her mother's fear. Her father expressed his intent to retire once his tour at the War College concluded; Renee dreaded this precipitous loss of status. To appease her mother, Sara remained in Newport the summer before her junior year of college, assisting Renee with yet another party instead of orchestrating gala events in Boston. One evening, as they worked on seating arrangements, they were interrupted by a knock at the door.

"I almost forgot," Renee said. She rose to answer the door. A place card remained in her hand. "Admiral Brant's son is on base for the summer. I invited him over for a drink. You should go up and change."

Sara rolled her eyes. Admiral Brant's kid would be the third son-of-an-acquaintance whom Renee had invited over that summer. Sara already resented the forfeiture of her internship. Having to deal with these intolerably boring men made Sara want to scream. That is, until Paxton walked into the room.

He wore fitted jeans, a dark blue blazer, and a Tag Heuer which peeked out from underneath the cuff of his collared shirt. He looked dignified without trying too hard and possessed an impish look despite his pronounced brow line and angular cheekbones. They chatted politely for about an hour, with Renee finding several excuses to run into the kitchen to fetch another unnecessary beer or glass of water or snack.

"I don't suppose you have any plans for the evening?" Paxton asked during one of Renee's retreats from the family room. "You can give me the local's tour."

"Anything to get out of here," Sara said, motioning to her mother in the next room. "I'm really sorry about that."

"Don't be," Paxton replied. "You are a pleasant surprise."

They'd been walking down Thames Street when Sara caught their reflection in a darkened storefront window and abruptly stopped.

"We look so attractive together," she murmured.

"What's that?" Paxton asked. She'd spoken too softly for him to hear.

"Nothing," she said. "Well, no. Not nothing. It's just, this feels right." She sighed and pressed her body into his, jumping up onto her toes to reach his parted lips. When he kissed her back, Sara thought she'd shatter into a million pieces.

"I entirely agree," Paxton said afterward, pinching her chin with his finger and thumb, a spontaneous gesture which would thereafter become their own unique expression of affection.

Paxton felt both solid and exciting. He loved the way Sara listened to him instead of trying to interject. The other girls he'd dated were too focused on themselves to fully appreciate his ambitions. Both his father and grandfather were admirals, and he well understood the legacy he protected. For Sara's part, Paxton's maturity thrilled her. He wasn't like the other guys she dated who aimlessly drifted through life without direction. She thought of her party planning business less and less as the summer progressed, and all but abandoned it when she returned to school in the fall. Paxton occupied her every thought. On Christmas Eve, he proposed with his grandmother's Ascher-cut ring, and they made plans to get married as soon as Sara graduated.

"Just promise me you won't be like the rest of them," Sara told Paxton as he wrapped her in his arms. "Not like my father was."

"What else could I possibly want but you?" Paxton said in reply. Sara allowed herself to sink into his solid frame, feeling as if she could melt into him entirely and make him an extension of herself.

Shortly after their engagement, however, Paxton learned that his ship's deployment schedule had changed, making a wedding the summer after

Sara's graduation impossible. They would either have to get married in the fall or postpone for another year.

"Long engagements raise suspicions," Renee cautioned, so by April, Sara and Paxton had decided on a fall wedding. She could always go back to school, Sara told herself. Except she didn't expect Paxton V., Caroline, and Bryce to arrive in such quick succession, nor did she expect the utter chaos the kids brought with them. With Paxton gone so often, Sara relished the distraction. She made friends quickly, as she always had, and threw herself into organizing social gatherings and playdates. Renee visited whenever she could. She now helped Sara throw her own parties and always reminded Sara to keep her eyes fixed on the future.

"It's hard at first," Renee reassured her. "You're low on the ladder for now. But don't forget who you are." Then, she'd add in a half-begrudging tone, "With Paxton, you'll even go farther than I did."

Yet her relationship with Paxton became more transactional as the years wore on. The kids wailed and acted out whenever Paxton went out to sea, then rebelled against his every request once he returned. He never seemed to take to his children. In fact, Sara couldn't recall a moment when he had voluntarily hugged any of them. Exhausted by the late hours he worked, he'd wave Sara or the kids away, asking whether it was too much to get ten minutes to himself. Most nights, he went out after work, returning long after Sara and the kids were in bed.

Whenever these moments struck, Sara planned another party. It didn't have to be elaborate—a simple barbecue or drinks with friends would suffice. She would sit arm-in-arm with Paxton, the sly grin returning to his face, his arm draped around her shoulders. Together, they would dazzle their guests, see themselves as others saw them. Sara and Paxton were never more in love, it seemed, than when they were in front of other people.

During the past year, though, it didn't seem like enough. Paxton abandoned her at parties and would return distant, unbuttoned, and clouded with bourbon.

"I don't need you reminding me what's at stake," Paxton would say when Sara cautioned him about his behavior. Sara cultivated a thousand excuses in her own mind—the stress of his job, the tedium of fourteen years of marriage, anxiety over his impending selection for commanding officer. Deep down, though, she feared he wanted something else, something Sara couldn't offer. He always said he'd never leave her or the kids, and Sara believed him, if only for the sake of his career. This reassurance didn't prevent Sara from dreaming of the afternoon when she found her mother on the closet floor. She felt vulnerable for the first time in her life and needed to regain control the only way she knew how.

Grant's affair really couldn't have arrived at a better time.

*

When Sara arrived, Emiko sat on Celia's couch underneath a landscape oil painting of horses grazing in a pasture. The other women from the wardroom herded around poor Emiko, making her shift uncomfortably on the stiff brocade sofa.

"Emiko," Sara said. "It's so good to see you." Emiko tilted her head like a confused puppy. A natural response, considering Sara and Emiko had barely exchanged three words during the eight-month period their husbands had been stationed together. In fact, none of the wardroom wives had ever exchanged any words with Emiko, assuming she spoke no English. When they invited Emiko to wardroom events, they sent text messages containing emojis rather than words:

6 @ 🌙 🏠 🍷 😣

Had they bothered to ask, they would have learned that Emiko was born in Berkeley and met Grant while she worked as an analyst for the State Department in Tokyo. As a second-year law school student at William and Mary, Emiko didn't have time to attend the endless array of parties these women hosted.

"Would you like a drink?" Bethany asked, ignoring the full glass of chardonnay Emiko held in her hand. "Something to eat?" She mimed an eating motion, which made Emiko break into a fit of laughter.

"My dear, you may want to start drinking, because we have some bad news for you," Celia said, kneeling in front of Emiko and taking her hand.

"Um, what's going on?" Emiko asked.

"Look, Emiko, there's a rumor going around that Grant—well, how are the two of you?" Celia asked, her voice wavering as she spoke. Sara sighed.

"Ce, may I?" Sara asked, kneeling and taking Emiko's hand from Celia's grasp. "Emiko, there's no easy way to say this. Bethany overheard something the other day that we thought you should know. One of the new officers onboard, a young woman, made advances on Grant."

"Excuse me?" Emiko pulled her hand away from Sara's.

"Another woman," Sara said more loudly. "Grant. Do you understand what we're saying?

"I speak English, you know," Emiko said.

"Good for you, sweetie," Celia said.

"Don't worry. We'll make sure the girl who's involved pays," Sara said.

They saw Emiko's chest rise and fall rapidly. She let her wine glass drop to the floor.

"You are all out of your minds."

"Oopsy," Celia said. "We have a spill. I'll get a towel."

"This must be hard to hear," Bethany said. "But I know what I heard."

Emiko stood abruptly and interrupted her. "Well, you heard wrong. And how racist are you all to assume I don't speak English?"

The other women diverted their gaze from Emiko and looked at each other quizzically.

"Didn't you meet Grant in Japan," Bethany said.

Before she could speak again, another woman sprinted into the room.

"Nicola's here!" The woman yelled. "She just arrived with one of the other female officers."

"Whatever game you're all playing, you can sure as hell leave me out of this." Emiko left, her departure eliciting no reaction from the rest of the group.

"Oh, I'm so nervous," Celia exclaimed, rushing back into the room. "I need to welcome her. Bruce can't know about this! And my rug! Can someone blot that?"

Sara moved to the edge of the room to get a better look at the girl. Sara paid attention to the way she moved with coltish strides from the front door, past the entrance to the den, and into the Farbish's kitchen. The girl cordially shook Commander Farbish's hand, then proceeded to the back patio where she joined a huddle of other younger officers Sara had never met, including another girl with a comically long face and a linebacker's build. Between the two of them, Nicola had to be the attractive one. Paxton joined the circle as well, nudging the homely girl to the side with his shoulder. She playfully nudged him back.

Paxton must be tipsy, Sara thought.

Sara looked back to the other girl and the way her auburn hair fell to the middle of her back and frizzed slightly in the humid air. She wore a white shirt dress—rather, the dress wore her. Even tied at the waist, it consumed her slender frame and hit her legs at an unflattering mid-calf length. The girl had high cheekbones, a slender nose, and wore little makeup, which Sara thought made her look unfinished. A pink tone emerged underneath her skin; the type of radiance only possessed by the young.

She's practically a child, Sara thought. Suddenly aware of her prolonged musing, Sara tossed back her shoulders and moved back to the center of the room.

"Relax, Ce," Sara said. "We have it completely under control. See if you can lead her in here. And Bethany, grab us a few bottles of wine, please. Red will do nicely."

Sara watched as Celia wandered to the back patio and greeted each of the girls. Celia gestured in the direction of the den, then retreated to the kitchen. The prettier one followed her into the house. The tall, heavy-set girl shook her head and remained by Paxton's side.

By the time the girl wandered into the den, the women formed a phalanx behind Sara, their glasses full to the brim.

"Hi," the girl said firmly, oblivious to the poisonous looks she received. "I wanted to come in and introduce myself. I'm…"

"We know who you are," Sara said. Her heart pounded so furiously, she felt lightheaded. "We know all about you. Like how you enjoy sleeping with other women's husbands."

The other women, stirred by Sara's boldness, edged around the girl in a circle, their glasses held high.

"Sorry, what?" The girl laughed as she replied.

"Don't play dumb!" Bethany said. "We're on to you."

"Whoa, you have the wrong idea," the girl said.

"Why, because you think we're stupid?" Bethany shot back. "We've seen your kind before. Little whores who think they can get away with anything."

"You don't get to mess with what is ours," another woman called out.

"Bitch," cried another.

"Ladies!" Sara said, quelling their rising voices, trying to steady her own. Renee's face involuntarily appeared in her mind. Every muscle in her body shook. "This is for Emiko."

"Who?" asked the girl as Sara tossed the contents of her wine glass into the girl's face. The dark red liquid ran down her neck and chest. The girl screamed, exhaling the wine in a mist, and raised her hands in a belated motion of defense. She tried to move forward, but Bethany tossed the contents of her glass directly onto the front of the girl's white dress. Monica spilled hers down the girl's back. The room erupted in shouts and flying liquid and flailing limbs.

"Whore!"

"Slut!"

"This is what you get!"

"Let me go!" The girl wailed as she pushed her way forward, attempting to force her way out of the stampede.

"Enough," Sara yelled. Though she still shook, she felt elated and giddy, as if she were hovering over the room, observing this messy, glorious scene from above. "Maybe now you'll know your place."

With a triumphant flourish, she spat directly into the girl's face.

"You are all out of your minds!" the girl screamed before sprinting out of the room and leaving trickles of wine in her wake.

"Oh my god!" Bethany exclaimed. "I can't believe we just did that!"

The other women chimed in, neighing with glee.

"Did you do it?" Celia asked as she waddled into the den. "Oh, my carpet!"

"We're going to need a lot of towels, Ce," Sara said. "And some carpet cleaner."

Sara followed Celia into the kitchen and refilled her wine glass with a still-shaking hand. She took a celebratory sip while surveying the officers gathered on the patio.

How neatly they liked to divide themselves up at parties like this, she thought: men outside, wives inside. None of that would matter anymore. She disrupted their order. The power she wielded behind the scenes was as important—more important, even—than the type the officers brandished. *I'll tell Paxton about this tonight*, Sara thought. *He'll have to respect me for it*. She watched him outside, deep in conversation with the homely girl.

Commander Farbish clapped his hands and waved for the guests lingering on the patio to enter the house. The group followed him in.

"Ah, Celia, Sara," Commander Farbish said as he entered the kitchen. "We're going to start our presentations to welcome the new officers in the foyer. Have you seen Ensign Bradford? She's the only one we're missing."

"Who?" Celia asked. Then, with a stupid grin added, "We saw Ensign Mattingly come through a few minutes ago, though. She left in a huff. It was very rude, Bruce."

"Celia's right," Sara added. "The new girl was just in the den. Honestly, to leave the party your commanding officer throws for you. Such audacity."

"No, no. We have two new female officers onboard. That's Nicola Mattingly," Commander Farbish said. He pointed out the kitchen window to the homely girl standing next to Paxton, leaning her shoulder into his and contorting her hideous face into a gummy smile. "I'm talking about Laura Bradford, the other Ensign. Bright girl." He lowered his voice and, somewhat conspiratorially, said "Senator Bradford is her mother, you know, so we'd better be good to her!"

Sara tensed and walked away from Bruce without responding. As she approached the window overlooking the back deck, she watched Paxton chat with the real Nicola. They stared into each other's eyes in a way that made Sara shake uncontrollably.

"Congratulations," Bethany said as she joined Sara at the window.

"Bethany," Sara asked, her mouth and throat suddenly feeling dry. "Exactly what did Demetri say the other night? Word for word, what did he say?"

"Demetri was saying that Grant was sleeping with the new girl."

"And you're sure he said Grant?" Sara asked. *Since when do they refer to each other by their first names?* Their husbands always referred to each other by their last names or job title or whatever uncouth nicknames they created for one another. "Are you sure there was no other noise in the background?"

"Oh, our house is always loud. But what else could I have heard?"

Sara listened to Bethany without removing her gaze from Paxton and Nicola. She stopped breathing altogether once Paxton lifted his hand to Nicola's face, and with his forefinger and thumb, lightly pinched her shapeless chin.

Sara let the wine glass slip from her hand. The solid crystal goblet splintered into shards upon impact, drawing the attention of everyone at the party.

Sara Brant should have been mortified by such a faux pas; at the very least, she should have appeared contrite and offered to help Celia with the clean-up. *Accidents only happen to the careless*, Renee would say. But Sara didn't care what Renee would say. Nor did she care about the other partygoers' stares or how they would whisper about her in the days to come.

She could only think how unrecognizable the remnants of the glass seemed now, an object that felt so firm within her grasp a mere breath beforehand, scattered in a bouquet pattern upon the cold, hard floor.

THE CURATOR OF
OBSCENITIES

We didn't bring any mortuary equipment with us on my last deployment. Not enough, anyway. No one on the ship thought to include it. Then we discovered the bodies, 127 of them. Migrants whose boats capsized in rough seas on their way to Italy or Greece. We pulled them all out of the water and used whatever was available to label the remains: duct tape, engineering tags, even red curling ribbon, the type used to decorate Christmas packages. The incident became infamous across the Navy, as all screw-ups do. That was over two years ago. By the time I had transferred to another command and started preparing for my second deployment, word had spread throughout the fleet, and my new ship had enough bags and tags onboard to accommodate five cruise ships' worth of human remains. This freed up our minds to focus on other preparations.

Namely, porn.

It started four months before our scheduled deployment date, when Petty Officer Gerbowicz got busted for downloading porn on the ship's network. Since my collateral duty onboard is Legal Officer, I attended the Captain's Mast to process Gerbowicz's paperwork. Admittedly, it was one of the more entertaining Masts I've seen.

Captain's Masts are supposed to be somber affairs. You're determining the future of someone's career. During this one, though, we talked about porn. In front of our female commanding officer. Hell, we even had to look at some of it, being evidence and all. To her credit, the CO dealt with the proceedings with her usual detached professionalism. She finally broke toward the end, though, asking the question everyone in attendance wanted to know: "We're in our homeport—why didn't you download this shit at home?"

I'm paraphrasing here.

Gerbowicz stammered on about hiding the porn from his wife, since she'd lose her mind and demand they go to a marriage counselor if she found out. Their marriage was fragile, so he *had to* (his words) download it on the ship. Next, he turned to the CO, and in the most ballsy move I've ever seen at a Mast, asked, "Ma'am, you said deployment readiness should be our top priority. Really, I was just following your orders."

The CO didn't like that. She reduced him in rank and docked his pay. Still, he had a point.

"Sam, what *do* we do about porn?" Kent, one of my roommates on the ship, asked me once the Mast concluded. As Gerbowicz's division officer, Kent had also attended the proceedings. We left the Mast together and headed to the wardroom, where the executive officer would be holding his daily operation brief. "We're going to be gone for eight months and I don't know about you, but I'm going to need to jack off at some point."

We grabbed seats toward the back of the wardroom next to our other roommates and Kent asked them the same question: "What are we going to do about...you know?"

One by one, panic crept across their faces as they listed reasons why they couldn't download porn at home.

Javier didn't want it in the house with his kids: "I have daughters, you know."

Horace worried his fiancée would freak: "This will be her first time with me gone on deployment. I can't test this with her."

Kent lived with his wife's parents, and they clearly had some boundary issues: "Man, my mother-in-law is all up in our stuff. She's all bent out of shape about us not having grandkids, so she went digging through our bathroom trashcan the other day to see if Viv is on the pill."

"Yeah, well, maybe if you leave a bunch of porn around the house you can finally get your in-laws to move out," Javier said. Kent flipped him off.

We whispered about potential solutions as the executive officer droned on in the front of the darkened wardroom. He conducted daily operations briefs to keep us apprised of global threats and news from the fleet, except he also showed us graphic images from war zones during every meeting. In this presentation, he revealed images of bloodied civilians sprinting away from an explosion in the background. Three women appeared in the forefront of the picture, clinging to each other as they ran. The impact of the blast had shredded their clothes, exposing their burned chests. Their mouths gaped open in expressions of agony and terror.

"Make no mistake about it, gentlemen," the XO said. "You may not see it directly, but this is the consequence of what we do."

"That's it," Horace said, hitting me on the leg. "We're all bringing our own laptops with us on deployment, right?" The XO noticed our side conversation and cleared his throat pointedly. We turned to face the front of the room for a few minutes, pretending to pay attention, then picked up where we left off.

"We chip in for a subscription to one of those online porn sites," Horace said quietly. "And designate one person who downloads all the content onto an external hard drive. We'll have an entire library at our disposal once we get underway. Reduce the risk of exposure to one person."

Kent and Javier snapped their heads in my direction. They argued that I didn't have to worry about a wife, or kid, or noisy mother-in-law peeking over my shoulder. I reluctantly agreed. Not because I wanted to, but the guys looked so pumped, I couldn't say no.

"Talia will be cool with this, right?" Javier asked. "Being an artist and all, she's all used to seeing naked people."

"We'll see," I said.

*

When I arrived home later that night, Talia was in the garage of the rented brick colonial we shared. We started dating almost two years ago, shortly after I returned from my first deployment, and moved in together a year later. She breathed life into the bland home with both her bright personality and the oeuvre of paintings in various stages of completion she left lying around each room. That night, I watched as she leaned over my workbench. My open toolbox rattled as she stabbed at a piece of aluminum with one of my screwdrivers. In her newest creation, she outlined a woman in thin, silver wire. She painted over the wire with thick, globby strokes, applied with a palette knife instead of a brush, making the subject's flesh appear veiny and textured. Mismatched buttons served as her eyes, frayed electrical cords for her hair, and dried wads of white and pale green bunched together in a V-shape between her legs. Talia continued to work, entirely unaware of my presence. I didn't disturb her, but smiled as I watched Talia wrinkle her nose and stick out her tongue in concentration. She wore a paint-splattered smock over a pair of leggings and one of my t-shirts that nearly reached her knees.

"Tal," I said. "I have a steel punch that can do that."

She didn't look up and continued to stab at the piece of metal with an explosive intensity, the kind of passion I only seemed to experience when I watched her work. We met at a time when it seemed like everything in my life was tainted in some way. Then came Talia, with all her ambition and life. Being with her makes me feel like, I don't know, maybe there's hope for me.

Five minutes elapsed. Then five more. Only then did I approach her and wrap my arms around her smocked waist. She shrieked.

"How long have you been there?" she asked.

"Long enough," I said. "Who's this?"

"Garbage girl," she said. "Working title, for now. I'm thinking my next collection will only use materials I find on the street."

Glancing over her shoulder, I saw two flattened discs, the remnants of the exterior of a Sprite can. Talia dimpled the surface of the aluminum and affixed a red pushpin in the center.

"Nice cans," I said.

She leaned back, pressing her soft body into mine. "What would I do without such wit in my life?"

"Run away with some rich dude," I said. "Live in a big house with an art studio and get commissions from all his rich friends. Sounds like a much better option."

"Nah, I'd rather toil in a rented garage with *Garbage Girl*," she said. "Help me clean up?"

"Horace had an interesting idea today," I said as we entered the house and proceeded to our bedroom to change—me out of my uniform, she out of her painting attire. "And I, uh, kind of need you to be cool with it."

"Sounds serious."

"Not really. I told you how we've started prepping for deployment, right? And the idea for how we would, um, acquire certain items came up."

"Like alcohol? You know I've been saving my empty bottles of mouthwash for you."

"Oh, I thought that was for Mouthwash Man."

"Quit while you're ahead, babe. Horace had an idea?"

"OK, so, it's porn, Talia. We agreed one of us would download a stash of porn for deployment and I would be the one to do it."

Talia broke into a forceful fit of laughter.

"You're not mad?" I asked.

"Not mad," she managed to say, wiping tears from her eyes. "What, were the other guys too scared to ask their wives?"

"Not everyone is as cool as you."

"Don't pander," she said. "Please tell me you aren't getting the real demeaning stuff. I couldn't live with myself knowing I shacked up with some caveman."

I smiled, lifted her off the ground as she reached to grab a sweatshirt off the floor, and tossed her playfully onto the bed. She released a peal of laughter.

"A complete neanderthal," I said.

After, tangled in the bed sheets with her lithe limbs, I drifted off and dreamed of looking out onto the open ocean—one of those stretches at sea when there's nothing in sight besides the slowly surging water and oppressive haze on the horizon. Suddenly, a body emerged, a bloated back rising from the water like some breaching sea animal. Another appeared. Then another.

I woke with a start and saw Talia glancing down at me, half propped up on one arm, her other hand on my chest.

"Hey," she said. "Are you ok? You were twitching like crazy."

*

The guys and I met up later that week to review our options. Horace had done some research and recommended CumHub.com as our primary vendor.

"Acceptable from a cost and quality perspective," he said gravely. The rest of us laughed at his serious expression. We agreed to a year-long, all-you-can-download subscription. But we all have our thing, and I wasn't about to do all the downloading without the guys' input. Not that I cared what got everyone else off, I just didn't want to be in the position of guessing everyone's preferences. It's like overseeing the music on a road trip. Only much more revealing.

"We each get five slips of paper," Horace announced, holding up an emptied, wide-mouth soda bottle which would serve as a make-shift ballot box. "After the XO's daily gorefest, we put our choices in the bottle."

"What is it with XO and those graphic-ass images?" Javier asked.

"Focus, Javi," Horace scolded. "No names, no judgment. Sam will be the only one to see it. Agreed?"

We all nodded.

Later that afternoon, the XO's brief featured images from inside a combat hospital, where medical staff forcefully restrained an elderly man while a doctor sawed through his leg below the knee. The man sat up, alert, his face contorted in agony. XO flipped to another image, revealing images of mangled, emaciated dogs lining the streets. Murmurs arose from the room; he hadn't shown us pictures of dead dogs before.

"We may be firing from a distance, but these are the consequences of what we do," XO said. "Come to terms with this now so you don't freeze up when it's time to engage."

*

After the brief, the guys transcribed their kinks on torn sheets of lined paper and crinkled them into little balls, placing their suggestions into the bottle

I'd left on my stateroom desk. I reviewed them later that night. Most requests were predictable—big tits, threesomes, an overwhelming number of requests for anal—though some shocked me: romantic scenes; bondage; one request for tentacle porn, which I didn't even realize was a thing. A few requests for some dark shit I'm not going to mention and I immediately threw away. One request got stuck at the bottom of the bottle and I couldn't get it out for a solid week. When I did, it read *sexy feet*.

Jokes ensued, of course. They called me the *Dirty Librarian*, *PervO*, *Porn King*. Javier used the shipboard engraver to make me a nametag with *Kink Master* listed as my job title. The asshole put it on my uniform when I wasn't paying attention, so I ended up walking around with it on all day. My favorite moniker, though, was *The Curator of Obscenities*. It added an air of sophistication to the deed, which I appreciated.

I took a methodical approach to downloading each video, creating a folder for each kink. Problem was, CumHub didn't have the best search functionality, something I realized after opening a video tagged as *Hot Moms* to discover a woman licking a hairy earlobe. This meant I had to watch every single clip to ensure there wasn't some weird revelation at the end—there's some twisted stuff out there. Combined with the overly dramatic moans, the guys' creepy voices, and the tinny soundtracks, it got old fast.

"That's such a fake face," Talia said one night as I brushed my teeth and simultaneously screeded an episode from a series called *The Gang Bang Chronicles*. "So are her breasts. And his penis. I hear they use prosthetic ones." She wrapped her arms around my neck from behind and kept watching the flashing images on the laptop screen. "This actually reminds me of some archival work I did in grad school."

"And how do I enroll in this school?" I replied.

"Hilarious. It was this internship with a private gallery. I dug through a bunch of stuff acquired by the collectors and had to document each object by style, year, distinguishing features. That sort of thing."

"Yes," I said. "Art preservation and horny friends' urges are completely the same."

The video ended and one called *Naughty Neighbors* started playing automatically.

"You joke, but archiving involves very little appreciation. You easily get desensitized to what you're cataloging. I remember looking at these beautiful artifacts—bronze busts, Romantic-era landscapes, indigenous shell jewelry—after a while, all I saw were tags. It cheapened it all."

"That's kind of the point," I said, stroking her arm lightly.

Reminders of my own spreadsheet annotations invaded my mind. *Male, no identifying documents, scar on left leg. Female, identifying document illegible.*

Dark hair, body decomposition prevents further identification. Child, boy, finger-prints not available due to hands and feet missing. I tried to focus on Talia's soft hair brushing my face instead. Inhaling the scent of acrylic paint and citrus shampoo, exhaling odors of salt water and decaying flesh.

"What is?" Talia asked.

"When you're away for so long, you don't want to think of anything too affectionately," I said. "Sex included. You put your emotions aside and get back to work."

"You can't just decide to turn off natural human responses," she said.

"You have to," I said. "It's the only way to get by."

"Interesting way of coping," Talia said, cringing as a woman with fuchsia braids on screen twisted her face in expressions indistinguishable from ecstasy or pain while a portly, grunting man penetrated her from behind.

Anal, I noted, then dragged the video icon to its proper file.

Later that night, I dreamt of bodies lined up in neat rows across the entire flight deck. Each possessed a red ribbon tied around the toe, the ends curling in festive spirals. The synthesizer-heavy soundtrack from *Naughty Neighbors* thrummed in the background. As I glanced down at one of the tags, all I could read were the words *sexy feet.*

*

Though the days felt long and arduous, the weeks leading up to deployment passed quickly. The crew dedicated hours each day to drills and maintenance, our bodies moving in unison while our minds floated elsewhere. I kept busy toiling over navigational charts and helping crew members write their wills and powers of attorney. The only thing punctuating the monotonous days were the screening parties where I'd show my roommates the highlights from the latest videos I downloaded. These always seemed to follow the XO's daily briefs.

Talia worked furiously, too, applying finishing touches to her collection. She planned to present her pieces in an upcoming art show down in the Outer Banks. Since the show coincided with my pre-deployment leave period, we rented a house on the water where we'd stay for the week.

One night, needing a break from staring at strangers' contrived screams, I ventured into the garage to watch Talia at work. Discarded objects littered the garage floor, including plastic bags, pebbles she had painted and laid out on a tarp to dry, a plastic snorkel sliced in half lengthwise, and pans of blue and green paint. As I approached, I tripped over a box of metal scraps from her latest foraging expedition. Talia gasped and turned abruptly.

"Sam," she said, stepping in front of the canvas. "I don't want you seeing this one."

"When have you been shy about your paintings?" I asked.

"I just don't want you looking at it."

"I'm sure it's great," I said, moving toward her and lifting her up playfully. She stiffened and strained against my grasp.

"I'm not messing around."

The seriousness in her voice jarred me, so I set her back onto the ground. Not before I stole a glance at the canvas.

A woman lay suspended in a pool of blue, clearly meant to be water, though Talia hadn't added dimension to the painting yet to indicate depth. Her skin looked pale and lifeless. She held a small bouquet of flowers, made from candy wrappers and plastic bags. She winked at the viewer. The spliced-open snorkel protruded from her lips.

"Oh," I said, turning from the canvas and back to Talia. She looked up at me with wide, frightened eyes.

"I should've realized earlier how insensitive this is. You know how wrapped up in my work I get. I wanted to talk to you about it first," she said.

"You don't have to hide stuff like this from me," I said. And I meant it. The painting elicited nothing from me except confusion. I mean, why the flowers?

"It's just, with everything you told me about your last deployment, and this one coming up," she said. "You're really not upset?"

"Of course not. I can't freak out every time I see a picture of someone..." I trailed off, largely because I didn't know if the woman in the painting was supposed to be drowned or not.

"I just didn't want to cause you to have some reaction or something," she said.

"Tal, you don't need to worry about me," I said. "What's this one called?"

"*Ophelia's Escape*," she said. "Get it?"

"Sure," I said, even though I didn't.

"Are you really all right?" she asked. I hugged Talia instead of answering, content that she didn't know the full story. The fresh splotches of paint from her smock soaked through my shirt.

Shortly after we had moved in together, Talia found an article online about my last ship finding the capsized migrant boats. She came to me in tears, asking me if I wanted to talk about it. I did. I wanted to tell her everything, to crumble in her lap and have her piece me together, like one of the subjects in her artwork. But that felt like too much pressure to put on her and a new relationship. So I said it wasn't a big deal. As far as she knew, I saw the wreckage from afar. Too much time had passed for me to come clean now.

I never told her I was the one who processed the bodies. How I worked two full days without sleeping, attaching make-shift tags to bloated corpses and disembodied parts. How I took pictures, documenting any physical attributes which could be used for recognition. Or how, for weeks after, I answered queries from migrant aid agencies, surveying pictures to see if the remains we found matched descriptions from family members. *A young woman with dyed red hair? A teenage boy with a purple birthmark on his left forearm?*

No one wanted the job. My boss volunteered me for it. Said I seemed solid enough to manage. And I did, mostly. Except when I noticed how four of the corpses, one woman and three smaller children, wore identical yellow windbreakers. It made me remember a trip I took to Disneyland with my family when I was six or seven, for some reason, when my mother made my brothers and I wear these tacky matching t-shirts for the duration of the trip.

To pick you out of a crowd in case we get separated, she said.

"I think these should be together," I told the Department Head supervising the effort.

Without warning, the heat and smell in the hangar overwhelmed me. I sprinted to the nearest trashcan I could find and heaved I could no longer stand.

"Get a hold of yourself," the department head hissed. "We're only taking inventory, for God's sake."

"Only inventory," I repeated. I took a sip of water, spat it out, and got back to work.

One child, female, wearing a yellow poncho, I typed into my spreadsheet.

*

A week before leaving on deployment, Talia and I drove to her art show. She assembled a few companion pieces into a collection she called *Found Women*. Her work received praise from most of the attendees, including a gallerist from Atlanta who gave Talia his card to discuss a potential sale. A columnist from a regional art magazine photographed her work and called it a "poignant reclaiming of female agency" and other expressions I didn't understand, but made Talia radiate with pride.

We grabbed dinner after the show and when we returned to the beach house, I dozed off on the couch. Images from XO's briefs dominated my dreams and, with disturbing vividness, mingled with scenes from the porn videos. Three women fleeing an explosion entwined themselves between the cast of the *Gang Bang Chronicles* while a doctor looked on, mid- amputation. Naughty neighbors cavorted in craters left by missile blasts as the fuchsia-haired woman pleasured herself amid the mangled remains of street dogs. Garbage Girl stood off to the side, her arms crossed, glaring at the scene disapprovingly. All along the dirt road, bodies emerged to the surface, as if the solid ground suddenly liquified. They revealed their backs as they rose, then rolled over, exposing their decaying faces. Moans rose and fell like a chorus, notes of terror braiding together in a melody of tormented, facetious pleasure.

I jolted awake when Talia gently shook my arm, half expecting to still be surrounded by the hideous visions of my dream.

"You were really out," Talia said. "Come on. I'll be outside. Join me."

I got up and found Talia standing at the far end of the balcony. The dark waters of the Atlantic shimmered behind her and the half-light of the waning moon cast a soft light over her long limbs, making her skin look as if it glowed from within. The evening breeze off the ocean caused her hair to lift and swirl in delicate strands. She looked like some ethereal creature, too perfect to be real.

And I just stood there, trying to reconcile the images from my dream with the one unfolding before me now. No emotion followed. No horror at the visions violating my dreams. No elation or arousal at the sight of Talia standing before me. I knew how I should respond to each, what action was expected, but no sensation drove those responses. Maybe I'd submerged everything too far within myself to bring back up. Maybe the only thing left to feel was this sinking sensation and the overwhelming nothingness that followed.

DEAREST

Every day for the past year, I walked past the same man sitting on a park bench in Farragut Square rattling his meager change inside a Big Gulp cup. His pitch altered with the seasons:

"Help a man stay hy-drate-ed! Ain't no summer like those in the district!"

"It's cold again, folks! Freezing out here. Spare whatcha got before heading into those heated of-fi-ces!"

His bellowed appeals and resonant tenor echoed off both the historic wrought iron and weathered stone buildings and the modern glass and chrome edifices standing as sentinels around the square. Most passers-by diverted their eyes to their phones or intentionally turned their heads. A few tossed dollar bills from their leather wallets before scurrying with their briefcases and totes into K Street offices. Even the statue of Admiral Farragut—the green weathered bronze sculpture looming nearly thirty feet above the eponymous square—seemed to divert his gaze from the surrounding squalor.

Sometimes the man brought cardboard signs. He had impeccable handwriting, a detail that belied his missing teeth and the layers of tattered rags he wore.

ITS RAININ' ITS POURIN'
CROWDSOURCE MY UMBRELLA

About a month later, he designed another sign which immediately grabbed my attention:

GOT GUILT??
Donate Here!!

I gave him twenty dollars for that one. I can hardly escape my own sense of entitlement while living in this city. Besides, as a marketing professional, I had an appreciation for his craft.

"Well done," I said as I fumbled with my wallet. "You do better work than some of my junior ad writers."

"Glad you like it," he replied. "Send them out here if you want Freddie to teach 'em a thing or two."

"I just might," I said.

In the months that followed, I dropped a few singles into his cup or would purchase an extra coffee and a bagel for him every time I passed. We'd exchange a few pleasantries, and I'd ask if he needed anything else. Eventually, our conversations became the highlight of my morning commute.

"Haven't seen you in a couple of days!" he said when after I took a week off over Christmas.

"Yeah, spent some time away," I replied, and handed him a bag of cookies I baked over the holidays and had brought with me from home.

"You had me worried," he said. With a wink and a grin, the man added, "Thought you left me for someone else." For a moment, I savored the feeling of being missed, even if it was only for transactional purposes.

Even if my meager daily offerings seemed pathetic against the sullen seasonal backdrop, watching his smile each morning brightened those dreary winter days. Freddie possessed the type of smile which stretched across his entire face—his eyebrows lifted, creases formed in the corners of both his eyes, and chapped flaps of skin folded back toward his ears whenever he saw me. The small gifts I gave Freddie probably benefitted my own ego more than his well-being—I understood the misery of being disregarded, even if being seen can bring about a different type of danger.

The crisp charms of winter evade downtown Washington, D.C. in January. In its place is the harsh foreboding chill of remembrance and soggy isolation. Gusts of cold wind funneled between buildings and gushed out in spontaneous, bitter torrents. The entire square appeared gray and sodden while the green statue of Admiral Farragut towered indifferently over the blots of faded fabric and weathered tents erected at the base of the statue. On the worst of one of these bleak mornings, one of Freddie's signs, propped at the marble base of Admiral Farragut's statue, once again caught my eye:

NAVY Man. Help me get my anchor ~~away~~ aweigh

"Never knew you were in the Navy," I said, fishing out all the cash that I had in my wallet: seven dollars. "I did my time in the Navy as well."

"Actually, this sign's a bit of a tall tale," Freddie responded. "I've found people give you more when they think you're a vet."

"Clever," I said, glancing down at the empty liquor bottles and American flag blanket peeking out of the garbage bag at Freddie's feet.

"The Admiral gave me that idea. I'm working with him now and he told me to write that." He lifted his hand, partially covered by the tattered remains of a filthy yellow glove, to point at the statue of Admiral Farragut.

"Well," I said as I walked away. "Hope he doesn't keep you too busy."

"Thank you, dearest. He wanted me to let you know he says hi."

"What did you say?" I abruptly stopped. A woman in a camel coat plowed into me as I turned to face him, diverting head-on into the steady stream of pedestrian traffic surging through the square. "Who told you to say that?"

Freddie merely pointed upwards again. "The Admiral did. He says you were the prettiest officer he had ever seen."

My limbs stiffened. I had walked through Farragut Square for years now, casually dismissing the link to my past it represented. Freddie's words awoke a dormant terror inside me. Especially calling me "dearest." Coincidence, surely.

Wordlessly, I ran from Freddie and into my office building. He called after me, saying something I couldn't and didn't want to hear. Our interaction had delayed my arrival, and I barely had time to throw my bag upon my desk, shrug off my coat, and grab my notebook before heading into Peter's office for our eight o'clock meeting.

Peter's office spanned the length of half of K Street and overlooked Farragut Square from four wide, floor-length windows. The morning sunlight glinted off of the silver picture frames and the crystal awards littering his desk. I squinted at the metallic haze it created as I stood in front of his open door.

"Vera!" Peter called and waved me in. My heels clicked noisily as I left the carpeted hallway and strode upon the hardwood floors which started at the threshold of his office.

"Grab a seat. Can Leah get you something? She's making me an espresso."

"I won't say no to coffee," I said.

"Let's get down to it." He slapped his hands on his desktop, causing the smiling faces in the picture frames—turned outwards and precariously perched on the very edge of his desk—to leap upward in response.

"We haven't really had the chance to work together before. But I've heard great things about you. How long have you been one of our marketing directors?"

"Almost ten years now," I replied. "After I left the Navy, I, uh, took a year off, then went to graduate school, joined the firm shortly thereafter, and have been here ever since."

"Ah, that's right, a Navy girl," Peter replied. "What did you do?"

"I was on a ship, an officer. I was on the USS *Farragut*, as luck would have it," I said, shaking my head to chase away Freddie's words from this morning: *the Admiral says hello.* "Guess there's no escaping him."

"Sorry?" Peter asked.

"Farragut was the name of the ship I was on when I was in the Navy. And Farragut Square is, um, right across the street," I said. "Funny coincidence, is all."

"Right," Peter replied. "I'm not one for city geography. Don't take the metro, have my own spot in the building's parking garage. But Farragut...I read somewhere the Navy always has a ship by that name. Superstition or something."

"More a matter of history, really. Farragut was the first American admiral," I said, watching as Peter turned toward his laptop. "Anyway, you mentioned you wanted to discuss a campaign with me?"

"Yes. This is the year you're looking to get promoted to partner, right?" He smiled when I said it was. "Your promotion year is difficult, as you well know. It always helps to have a big-ticket account to your name. Which is why I called you in. But before we get into that, do you have a family?" He motioned to the blonde figures smiling at me on his desk.

"Well, yes, my parents live outside of Philly. I try to take the train to see them every month."

"No, not that. I meant kids? Husband?" Peter asked, then added, "Or, you know, spouse. Partner-person."

I looked down again at the pictures guarding the edge of Peter's desk: two girls and a boy, none of whom looked no more than ten, standing at the bottom of a ski lift; a slender woman with large diamond jewelry and wavy blonde hair sitting on the steps of a brick porch and holding a plump, drooling baby; a blond gangly boy with missing front teeth hugging a golden retriever.

"No. Nothing like that," I said, not mentioning the divorce I finalized six months ago.

"Well, then," Peter clapped his hands. "No one to miss you when I steal you away for the next three months. I'd like you to lead our newest campaign!"

I got to work right away and spent the rest of the day staffing my team and building out our approach based upon the few client documents Peter sent my way. The new challenge served as a welcome distraction from the morning. Freddie's words and the uneasiness they stoked sunk into the recesses of my memory.

"Call your parents now so they don't report you missing!" Peter called as he passed by my office at 2:30 that afternoon, his briefcase and coat in hand.

Darkness shrouded the city when I departed the building at seven, stepping into the cruel slap of bitter wind funneling through the buildings lining both sides of the street. Farragut Square seemed to transform at night. An uneasy tension enveloped the area. Masses of blankets draped over and tucked around benches, creating make-shift tents on the street. Commuters held their bags more closely and intentionally avoided eye contact. Amber streetlights cast amber light from above, causing pedestrians to drag long shadows on the sidewalk behind them. An umbra obscured Admiral Farragut's face, as if he closed his eyes in a dismissive slumber.

Freddie leaned against the metro entrance, wrapped in layers of dirty towels and a sleeping bag with a broken zipper. A man in a dark coat and charcoal colored beanie hunched next to Freddie in conversation, his face wrapped a gray scarf. He darted away as I approached.

"There you are, dearest!" Freddie called. "Late one for you!"

"Yeah," I called back. There it was again: *dearest*. It had been so long since I felt the latent terror that word had elicited.

"You'd better find someplace to get inside tonight," I said. "It's too cold out here."

Freddie smiled. "I was just talking to the Admiral, ya know. That was him who just ran away. Said again how you were the prettiest officer he ever did see."

"Who told you to say that?" I asked, overwhelmed by the inexplicable sensation of sweating despite the cold.

A thin current of metro commuters flowed around us both at a distance.

"The Admiral. Like I told you. He just left. He said he returned to check up on you."

"Stop it."

"What I'd say?"

"You know what, it's best if you stop talking to me."

I darted into the gaping mouth of the metro entrance, glancing over my shoulder with every third step. I was overreacting. Freddie was drunk and telling wild stories to pass the time. That's all.

"You're safe," I said as soon as the metro doors closed, counting my breaths, just as the doctor told me to do. Then I repeated, "Stop being ridiculous. You're safe."

*

Back at home, I poured myself a glass of wine, then another, and called Mary, my roommate from when we served together on *Farragut*. Our conversations and visits felt disjointed in the past few years, punctuated by admonitions she always directed toward one of her three children. Tonight, Mary managed to put all her kids to bed for the evening and spoke to me without interruption. She congratulated me on the new campaign and updated me on her kids' latest attempts to fray her final nerve. Her voice assumed a different tone when I told her about Freddie.

"Let me get this straight. There's a homeless man living outside your office who is sending you messages from Admiral Farragut?" she asked. We both laughed. I detected the concern lingering in her voice, though, so I didn't tell her about the man I saw lingering around him by the metro station. Truthfully, I started to doubt I saw another person there at all.

"I know how it sounds. I'm not having a breakdown. Or another one, I guess. But something about it really creeped me out, Mary. Like I'm unable to escape the past. And I mean that literally: that damn statue is right there and now I have some poor man saying things that remind me so much of.... Does any of this make sense?"

"Look, I know you're not crazy," she replied. "You must trust yourself not to be as well. You had a hell of a time on that ship. I lived through it with you. You've had your ups and downs since then. Terry isn't coming back for you."

"Don't," I said. "I don't want to hear his name."

"I'm sorry. I get it, but you must trust that it's over now, Vera. Let it stay in the past. Unlike my children, the past doesn't bite."

"No," I said, draining the contents of my wine, watching burgundy-tinted remnants of liquid bleed down the side of the glass in slow-moving rivulets. "But it can hurt like a bitch."

"Maybe you should talk to someone," she said softly.

"You know I have," I replied. "But it just keeps coming back, you know? Sometimes I'm relieved it does. That means I didn't make it all up. Like everyone thought I did."

I closed my eyes, weary from the day's excitement, and instantly heard a voice emerge from the recesses of my brain—male, authoritative, and sharp: *This is the type of thing that can ruin a man's career. Are you sure you aren't overreacting?*

Could I ever be sure?

*

That next morning, and for most mornings throughout the rest of January and February, I avoided the metro in favor of driving to work. I told myself it made more sense to drive. I left the office so late in the evening that it was probably safer. Shame piqued me in those rare moments I allowed myself to admit I drove to avoid seeing Freddie.

The grueling pace of the campaign left little opportunity for self-reflection, though. I arrived at the office before eight in the morning, and never managed to leave before ten in the evening. Peter seemed to vanish every time I needed him to weigh in on a decision, only to reappear with a vague criticism requiring significant rework from our team. When I asked him about it, he merely shrugged and slapped me on the back: "You can figure it out. That's why we're going to make you a partner one day!"

Somewhere during the haze of spending nearly all my waking hours and weekends at the office, I managed to lose sight of the anxiety I felt about passing Freddie on the street. I still didn't take the metro, but occasionally managed to work up enough courage to venture out onto K Street for coffee breaks.

During one such trip with Cindy, one of my colleagues, I spotted Freddie. He had moved from the square to the K Street sidewalk and had transformed a bench into a cave of blankets and tarps. Only his eyes and nose were exposed. His eyes rolled back in a dreamlike state. A lanky, hunched, and hooded figure crouched beside him, nudging him gently.

"Long time, dearest," Freddie called as we passed by. His voice sounded weak, nearly vanishing in the rush of traffic and gusts of wind.

"Did you hear that?" I asked.

"That homeless guy moaning?" Cindy replied.

"Never mind," I said.

On our way back to the office, we passed by Freddie again. He sat alone, his companion having vanished. Freddie grew animated when he saw us, waving his arms and lumbering from his hut. He paced erratically in front of the bench.

"I have to tell you something, miss. It's real important." His voice slurred strangely, and he staggered as he approached us.

"Not now, Freddie. I need to go," I said, trying to act unperturbed.

"Do you know him?" Cindy asked, quickly retreating away from Freddie and toward the safety of our office.

"It's the Admiral!" Freddie shouted. "Look, miss, I don't know what he's about, but he's been asking for you and I don't like it."

He grabbed my right arm, causing me to jolt backwards and spill coffee down the sleeve of my jacket, staining his yellow gloved hand.

"Let go!" I pulled my arm back and took off toward the building. Freddie followed.

"No, you don't understand. We need to talk."

As I ran into the lobby, two of our building security guards rushed out and grabbed Freddie by the arms. I paused to look back, watching Freddie struggle to push them away.

"Get inside," one guard ordered.

"Go easy," I said, watching as the other security guard wrestled Freddie back outside. "There's something wrong with him today."

"Inside!" the other ordered.

About an hour later, the security guards met me in my office with a police officer following them. They asked me to relate the events of the morning as well as any other previous interactions I had with Freddie.

"Did something else happen?" I asked, realizing their line of interrogation exceeded the scope of today's encounter.

The officer looked at the security guards then closed his notebook.

"Freddie, as you referred to him, is Mr. Frederick Williams. He had ID on him. Looks like he overdosed. He started seizing after he grabbed you earlier, so we sent him to National."

"Overdose?" I asked. "I've seen him drunk before, but never high. That I could tell at least."

"They all have a trigger," the police officer said with a shrug. "The cold sometimes does it. Causes people to get desperate."

Later that evening, I called the hospital to check up on Freddie's status, but staff wouldn't reveal any of his information since I wasn't a family member. I couldn't tell if I wanted him to recover. I hated myself for the momentary relief this gave me. Regardless, I ventured out of the office for more frequent breaks, peering into every blanketed mound to see if Freddie had returned.

I never saw him again.

*

By early March, a cold but humid fog had descended over the city, making the sidewalks slick with condensation. Walking outside felt like putting on a still-wet bathing suit. A light blue haze hung over the square when I commuted to work in the mornings, and daylight stretched its cramped limbs further and further into the evening as if to cautiously test out the boundaries of how far it could go. Although most days were still wet and bitter, portents of spring appeared subtly and in unexpected ways: salt strips abating from the roads, rain flowing from sidewalk cracks and into sewer drains like tiny streams, boisterous chirps from the robins gathering in alleyways.

Hope no longer felt foolish.

Around this time, the marketing campaign wrapped up. Our team held a small celebration in the office, jovially sipping slightly acidic wine from clear plastic cups while Peter attended the official launch party with the client. The team scattered around eight. I retreated to my office to respond to a few emails long neglected due to the final surges of the campaign launch. Around eleven, I finally looked up from my work. Habituated to the loneliness, eerie groanings, and absurd silence of the office after hours, somehow three hours evaporated in front of my keyboard.

I packed up my work bag and shut my office door, watching the motion-sensing lights snap on as I continued down the empty corridor and to the elevator lobby. The void felt strangely comforting now. I braved the solitude alone, brazenly and triumphantly stepping into the elevator that carried me down into the parking garage underneath the building.

My victory proved to be short lived. When I reached my car, I glanced up at the parking tag tucked into the driver's side visor, noticing my monthly parking pass had expired. I would have to pay at the parking kiosk before exiting the garage.

The parking kiosk resided in a long rectangular vestibule, surrounded on three sides by glass, with a single glass door providing the only entrance or exit to the space. I left my car idling directly in front of the door and jumped out with only my credit card in hand. Inside the vestibule a robotic voice emanated from the kiosk, repeating "Please insert your parking ticket" with the urgency and intensity of a fire alarm.

As I waited for the machine to spit out my card, I heard a creak and caught the door swing open from the corner of my left eye. I started, unaware of anyone else remaining in the entire building, let alone the parking garage.

"Hello, dearest," he said.

I froze, enveloped by panic.

That voice. I identified it long before I turned to examine the figure before me. Wiry and tall, slightly stooped. I peered into his face, trying to reconcile it with the features I once knew. Hollow cheekbones and a prominent jaw, both covered by dark stubbled flecked with white. He wore a charcoal gray beanie, pulled low over his forehead and partially obscuring his deeply set eyes.

Could that really be him? I wondered. I doubted my memories for far too long to rely on them.

But his voice. That I would remember until my dying day.

"Terry?" I asked. "Terry, is that you?" I stammered again.

"Maybe," he said.

"What are you doing here?"

Terry remained silent, smiling the twisted smile which for years had prevented me from closing my eyes at night.

"What are you doing here?" I repeated. "You know you're not supposed to be anywhere near me."

"Didn't you get my messages?" He asked.

"What messages?" I asked. "You know you're not supposed to contact me."

"The ones from Freddie, of course," Terry said. "Don't you know, I told him I was Admiral Farragut when we first met. Thought you'd pick up on the reference. The poor drunken fool, I think he believed me."

"You...you were the one telling him to say those things." The hooded figure next to... Freddie.

Of course.

Every incident I attempted to repress from the past decade streamed through my head with immense, glaring clarity and violently collided into the reality I constructed in my current life: the cryptic messages Terry would write on my car window; the notes I'd find in my purse when I thought I was out alone, in my kitchen when I thought the apartment was empty. When I awoke in my stateroom on the ship in the middle of the night to find him standing over my bed.

You are the prettiest officer I've ever seen, his first note read. I was twenty-four at the time, stupid, thinking of this note from a much older officer as a harmless flirtation.

Don't you dare play with me. I will find you, read the last note, the one that appeared on my windshield while I was visiting a friend in another state.

My breathing grew rapidly, though it felt remote and surreal, as if my chest existed separately from my body.

"Didn't you like them, dearest?" Terry asked. "It's been far too long since I sent you a message."

"Don't come any closer. There are cameras all over this building." I cringed listening to my quivering voice. There were cameras, weren't they? The car was right there. If I could only get past him.

"Those cameras?" Terry gestured up toward a small white cylinder bolted to the ceiling above his head and roughly half a stride in front of him. I shifted my eyes up in a sequence of short glances, too terrified to look away for longer than the duration of one of my frantic heartbeats. The camera pointed away from the door and toward the payment kiosk. From that angle, it captured my every motion while Terry remained behind the lens, completely out of view.

He always knew how far to go. I was the only person within view: a frantic woman reacting to something invisible.

"They won't see me, dearest. Which means no one will believe you," he said. "Just like last time. Everyone thought you made it all up, you know. Remember all the things they said about you afterward?"

He clucked his tongue in mock censure.

"They believed me enough to give me a protective order against you."

"That's long expired now. Sure, they forced me to retire early. They didn't press any charges and I still got all my benefits. Kicked you out, though. Sent you to that hospital so you wouldn't try to hurt yourself again." He let out a short, mirthless laugh. "I think I got the better deal."

I frantically glanced side to side. The expansive bottom floor of the parking garage, completely deserted for the evening, stretched out on all sides, promising escape. Yet thick glass walls boxed me in on all sides.

"You need to leave," I said. Terry merely stood and stared back, solemnly shaking his head. My card remained half consumed by the machine, causing it to release high-pitched pleas for attention that reverberated, unnoticed, throughout the tiny space.

"You really should've listened to Freddie, you know. He practically told you I was here, but you ignored him. You'd think you'd be more sympathetic."

"What did you do to him?" I asked, fighting the wave of nausea rising in my stomach. "He did what you wanted, why would you hurt him?"

"Think he figured something was up in one of his sober moments. Said he was done passing along messages. I had to show him there were consequences for betraying me," Terry said. He bared his teeth and squinted his eyes into a vicious expression. "You both needed to be taught."

I stepped backwards cautiously, certain he'd spring forward at any moment, until I collided with the glass wall at the farthest corner of the vestibule. Terry remained impassive.

"Terry, it's been over ten years," I said. The words left my throat like the garbled end of an echo. "Move on, for God's sake! Haven't you done enough?"

"Oh dearest, I'll move on when you do," he said. "The better question is whether I'm real at all. People thought you were crazy back then. Still do."

I involuntarily traced the inside of my wrist, feeling the raised bumps running down my forearm, barely palpable through my thin silk shirt. They had almost faded.

"No," I said. "I know what happened. You need to leave."

"Not before you come over here and touch me," he said. "Come on. Try it. See if I'm real or if you're going crazy again."

He stood still, so still, daring me to move with his impassiveness. I wanted to stride toward him with my arms outstretched. To prove to him that he couldn't control me any longer. Instead, my hands clawed desperately against the cold glass wall behind me.

"Just as I thought. You can't be bothered, just like the old times. Here I am, trying so hard to get your attention, but you still think you're too good for the likes of me. Just like before when you flung yourself in front of me and tossed me away."

"I never did!" I shrieked and stepped forward with a fury that momentarily paralyzed all sense of reason. "Never, not for a moment. I know exactly what happened!"

"Don't you dare tell me what happened," he bellowed back.

I recoiled in response to his outburst and crumbled to the floor more violently than if I had been struck. Terry laughed at my response.

"You led me on, acting like you were too good for me, too smart. That I was just to be fooled with. And you thought you'd get away by telling all sorts of lies about me. Making the Navy put up an invisible fence, as if that would make me disappear."

He paused and flashed a cold, triumphant smile. "No. It doesn't work like that. I warned you not to mess with me. Now you get to know how it feels to always be thinking of someone."

As he finished his sentence, he lurched forward, springing like a snake ready to strike. I threw my arms over my head, as if to shield myself, shaking and sobbing uncontrollably, startling myself with the repellent sounds that emerged from my mouth.

"Don't worry," he said. "I'm not going to hurt you, dearest. But I'll be wherever you are. Watching as you get your groceries with those cute little yellow bags, or when you head to Penn Station for monthly treks to see your folks. Just like I did the night Scott stormed out of your old townhouse and went to that bar down the street. I sent him a beer from across the bar, you know. Poor bastard. I knew just how he was feeling."

That was the night I told Scott I wanted a divorce. I told him that I married him to feel secure without realizing I never actually would. That he couldn't help me. That I couldn't trust him or anyone else. We fought, but it made no difference—fear had stripped away my willingness for Scott's affection. Anxiety flared within my chest too vibrantly. I had no capacity to pretend to feel something I didn't. Scott hadn't reached the point of resignation yet. He pleaded, yelled, and pleaded some more. Offered to go to counseling with me. Told me I was letting my past destroy our future. Turns out the past bought him a drink that night.

"Maybe one day I'll get impatient," Terry continued. "Like that time outside of your apartment when I had to smash your windshield to get your attention. I hate it when you make me do dramatic things like that. Maybe I'll have to punish you like poor Freddie. Or I might just get bored and leave you alone. But this much I do know. We belong together. And I'll always be with you. In person," he held out his hands to emphasize his point and slowly backed away to the door. "Or in your mind."

With that, he walked backwards out of the vestibule, grinning at me the entire time, and disappeared around a corner of the parking garage.

I don't remember anything after that. Overwhelmed by emotion or deprived of oxygen from hyperventilating, I must have blacked out.

When I came to, I found myself in the driver's seat of my idling car, unsure of how much time had elapsed. Dazed and shaking, I slowly regained my awareness and noticed the alarms violently chiming throughout the vehicle. Blurry forms and shadows gradually coalesced into discernible landmarks.

The soft glow of amber streetlights illuminated the scene in front of me. I had somehow turned the wrong way into I Street, drove onto the curb, and crashed into a stone marker lining the boundaries of Farragut Square. My windshield wipers dragged wildly across the glass even though it wasn't raining. I traced a trail of crusted vomit down the front of my coat with a trembling hand.

Directly ahead stood Admiral Farragut, illuminated by a series of upward pointing, faintly flickering bulbs. His head tilted to the left, casting his apathetic, verdigris-crusted gaze into the distance, willfully overlooking the commotion below.

COMEBACK

Scene opens in darkness. Sounds of explosions, screams, the crunching of metal, and radio calls for assistance are heard, but nothing appears on stage.

Act I

The curtains part, revealing DESSA *in the hospital bed. She's surrounded by baskets of flowers and arrangements of fruit and desserts. She lies unconscious. A heartbeat monitor beeps steadily, but the pace seems slower than it should.* CORPSMAN *comes to check* DESSA's *chart. He looks at it, checks her vitals as she sleeps, then turns to the audience and speaks.*

CORPSMAN. Act I. Establishing Safety.

CHORUS OF DOCTORS *enter, their heads bent over their charts. They are all men, or appear to be, and are similarly attired in white lab coats, thick glasses, hair slicked back, stethoscopes slung around their necks. They stop center stage, standing directly in front of where* DESSA *lies, and snap their heads up from their charts in unison.*

CHORUS OF DOCTORS. Onward with our rounds!

DOCTOR 1. Another day goes by—

DOCTOR 2. Another TBI.

CHORUS. Onward! Onward with rounds!

DOCTOR 3. War's long trail of destruction—

DOCTOR 4. Unfolds before our eyes.

DOCTOR 5. Frightened, half-charred patients—

DOCTOR 6. Who trust us with their lives.

DOCTOR 7. But...

DOCTOR 8. Only so much we can do.

DOCTOR 9. Sadly, most never pull through.

CHORUS OF DOCTORS. Onward, onward with rounds!

DOCTOR 10. We bring back patients, part by part.

DOCTOR 1. This job's not for the faint of heart.

DOCTOR 2. Another day goes by—

DOCTOR 2. Look!

DOCTOR 3. Another TBI.

CHORUS. Onward! Onward with rounds!

HEAD PHYSICIAN: Pop quiz—what are the stages of a traumatic brain injury?

DOCTOR 1. Coma!

DOCTOR 2. Vegetative state!

DOCTOR 3, *yawning*. Minimally conscious.

DOCTOR 4. Post-traumatic amnesia?

DOCTOR 5, *slapping* DOCTOR 6's *rear*. Inappropriate behavior!

DOCTOR 6, *looking around in a bewildered manner*. Confusion?

DOCTOR 7, *reaching over to slap* DOCTOR 5 *across the face*. Automate and Appropriate!

DOCTOR 8, *shouting*. Purposeful!

DOCTOR 9, *shouting loudly*. Purposeful AND Independent!

CHORUS *cheers as they complete the sequence.*

DOCTOR 5, *whispering behind* HEAD PHYSICIAN's *back*. Cast your bets, folks! What are we going to see in bay 22?

CHORUS *debate amongst themselves. Their voices jumble together.* DESSA *stirs in the background.* Here's the patient the corpsmen were talking about!

DOCTOR 7. Look at her chart. Does that name sound familiar?

DOCTOR 8. Dessa Daniels? The child actress? How on earth did she get here?

DOCTOR 9. I loved her in *Fire and Ice*!

DOCTOR 10. I must have seen *The Secret Room* nine times as a kid.

HEAD PHYSICIAN. My children were all obsessed with her. Must have made me watch *Night of the Monsters* a thousand times.

DOCTOR 1. Haven't seen her name recently. Thought she was done with show business.

DOCTOR 4. Or the other way around.

DOCTOR 2. Was she doing some kind of USO thing?

DOCTOR 3. I don't think so. She's listed as Captain Goddess Daniels.

DOCTOR 5. Imagine going through life with that name…

DOCTOR 6. That doesn't matter when you're famous.

DOCTOR 7. Prospects must be slim if she joined the Marine Corps.

DOCTOR 8. How on earth did she get here?

HEAD PHYSICIAN. Enough gossip. What does her chart say?

CHORUS. Suffered multiple pelvic, rib, and leg fractures and head injuries following an IED attack on her convoy. Was evacuated to Landstuhl until she was stable enough to transfer to Walter Reed. Patient demonstrates symptoms of post-traumatic amnesia.

DOCTOR 6. Yes! Pay up, guys.

HEAD PHYSICIAN. What else does the chart say?

CHORUS. Patient's story is inconsistent with what was discovered at the scene of the attack.

HEAD PHYSICIAN. That's not unusual, considering the severity of her head trauma. Make a note to work through this during her rehabilitation.

CHORUS. Another day goes by, another TBI!

HEAD PHYSICIAN. On to the next patient...

CHORUS. Onward! Onward with rounds!

CHORUS OF DOCTORS *exits.*

ANGIE *enters. She possesses a shock of artificially red hair and is dressed in a leopard print jacket, an orange dress, and sky-high, purple heels. Shiny gold bangles clatter on both her wrists. She gestures wildly, revealing a flash of gold rings on her hand and long, bright red nails. She surveys the room and shakes her head. Then she jumps and clutches her chest. She looks as if she's about to cry, but composes herself, bites her lip, and proceeds to address the audience.*

ANGIE. Jesus, Mary, and Joseph, I hardly recognized her. You can't blame me, what with her her skull shaven and her face looking like an engorged eggplant. I hope they have a good plastic surgeon on staff.

DESSA, *waking. Her voice is raspy, her speech stilted and slow.* Angie? Angie, is that you?

ANGIE. Hi, honey. I came as soon as I could. I didn't bring you anything, though not that you need any more waist thickeners in here.

DESSA. I have enough of these...these...things.

ANGIE. Whatever you do, don't eat them all. Your metabolism is slower than a geriatric tortoise.

DESSA. It's good to see you.

ANGIE. Is it?

DESSA. Yeah. It helps to see a...a...

ANGIE. Friend? Familiar face?

DESSA. Yes. That.

ANGIE. What's going on, honey?

DESSA. I'm forgetting things, Ang. Not the thing itself, but the...oh...the thing you call it...

ANGIE. Words?

DESSA. Yes. Words.

ANGIE, *turning to the audience.* Oh boy. This will not play well in an interview. (*Turning back to* DESSA.) It's ok. You need to give yourself time to heal. But while you're laying here, I'd love to talk about my plans for you.

DESSA. Oh no.

ANGIE. You're going to love it. Get ready, because today, honey, is the first day of your.... Are you ready? Today's the first day of your...COMEBACK!

DESSA. Angie, please. My head...

ANGIE. Are you excited? Tell me you're excited.

DESSA. I'm on too much Dilaudid to be excited.

ANGIE, *looking at her IV bags*. You don't know words, but you remember Dilaudid? They did give you the good stuff, though, didn't they?

DESSA. It doesn't feel like it. I still have this...this...

ANGIE. Pain? Where?

DESSA. Everywhere, Ang. Everywhere. I just need to think of something else. Be someone else.

ANGIE. Honey. I'm so sorry. Can I get you anything?

DESSA. No. You here is enough. (DESSA *sits up in bed and addresses the audience directly. Her speaking cadence improves and her voice is clear*) Angie has been my manager since, well, for as long as I can remember. She terrified me the first time I met her. We were in her office in New York. My mom had my arm in this vice grip the entire elevator ride up to her office. Which was on the top floor, naturally. As Angie always said...

DESSA and ANGIE, *in unison*. It's the best or nothing, baby.

DESSA. My mom told me, "Behave yourself. Ms. Fangonella represents the biggest names in this business. If you mess this up, you'll be doing your homework by candlelight because our electricity's probably going to be turned off."

ANGIE, *turning to the audience*. Seeing her lying there, her body broken to bits, I couldn't help but remember her face the first time I saw Dessa. She was with that awful mother of hers. Always hovering, that one. In my four decades in the business, I'd seen my fair share of stage moms rotate through the Angie Fang Children's Talent Agency. Hands down, Dessa's mother was the worst.

DESSA. What's this about a comeback, Ang?

ANGIE. OK, so—! (*Digs through her purse*) Wait a moment, I have it all written out, let me just find it...

DESSA, *addressing the audience*. Angie's never led me astray, in my career, or in life. She helped me get one role after the next, coached me through each. Even later, after most of my prospects dried up, she helped me get back on my feet. Wrote me a great recommendation to Tisch. Suggested I do theater for a while, which I loved. She always thought I'd return to films one day. She didn't think I'd take a completely different path.

ANGIE, *addressing the audience*. Watching Dessa in her first commercial was magical. The kid shoved spoonful after spoonful of mushy pasta into her mouth, all while making her eyes appear as big as friggin' dinner plates. She seemed to enjoy it, too, never broke her expressions until after the direct shouted "Cut!" And she spit out the half-masticated paste into a bucket right below her seat. Even between takes, she beamed. Must've been at it for nine, ten hours that day. Ah, the golden days of relaxed child labor laws.

Anyway. As soon as the director wrapped the shoot, Dessa vomited. All over herself. Her mother was furious, whisked her off in a huff. Later, I asked her why she kept eating that cold goop instead of spitting it all out. She looks at me and, I'll never forget this, says she got lost in her character. Said she created a character for the role: a little girl named Beth whose mother was at a PTO meeting so her father made dinner for her. He couldn't cook well, so he heated up the pasta and spoke with her about her day. Said she wasn't smiling at the canned bullshit in front of her, she was smiling at her dad's jokes, content with the time she got to spend with him. That's why she forgot she was acting and not really eating. Five years old and she's coming up with that for a thirty-second television ad. She didn't even have a speaking role. At that moment, I knew this one was special. She was going places.

DESSA, *to the audience.* Role after role followed. Angie couldn't book me fast enough. It eliminated all possibilities of a normal childhood, but who cared? I got to create a new life for myself every time I stepped on screen. Escape for a little while. It was better than my reality.

ANGIE, *to the audience.* I never realized how badly Dessa needed these parts. One time, we got caught up in contract negotiations with the studio over her next role. Ended up in legal limbo for a few months. The way Dessa behaved while we waited, it terrified me. She refused to eat, screamed when her mother tried to get her out of bed. Wouldn't speak with anyone unless you told her it was for an audition. Nine years old and she's moping around like a despondent method actor.

That's when I started to wonder whether I was doing more harm than good. God forgive me, I didn't stop pushing her. She was my most lucrative client. And she seemed to really want to perform. It makes sense, in retrospect. ANGIE *pauses, visibly moved.* But I missed all the signs. I underestimated the pressure she was under. And I've spent my life trying to make it up to her ever since.

DESSA. The better I did, the worse things seemed to get at home. Mom started demanding more of me. Telling me the money I made was the only way we'd be able to survive. To keep our house. I believed her, of course. I had no idea how much things cost. I didn't realize how much of my acting paid for Mom's coke habit.

ANGIE, *turning back to* DESSA, *who returns to her hospital bed.* OK, so, for your comeback. We'll hire a film crew to document your recovery. Do a few interviews with entertainment magazines, the talk-show circuit when, you know, your face is a little less swollen. I must admit, honey, I never thought much of this military thing of yours, but it does play well to a nostalgic audience. A real patriotic schtick. People will love it.

DESSA. Ang, let's not get too, um, uh...

ANGIE. I haven't even gotten to the best part! We—

CHORUS OF DOCTORS *enters. They buzz around her in a flurry of activity, taking* DESSA's *blood pressure, temperature, checking her monitors, and shining lights in her eyes as they speak.*

ANGIE. Go ahead and interrupt. Not like we were in the middle of a discussion.

HEAD PHYSICIAN. How are we feeling today, Captain Daniels?

DESSA. Like I got blown up.

HEAD PHYSICIAN. Blood pressure?

CHORUS. Stable!

HEAD PHYSICIAN. Temperature?

CHORUS. Normal!

HEAD PHYSICIAN. Motor responses?

CHORUS, *turning the palm of* DESSA's *one hand not in a sling upward and pressing down, rapping her on the elbow afterward.* Observed weakness!

DESSA. Ouch!

CHORUS. Delayed response!

HEAD PHYSICIAN. Ah, let's not forget the most important question...

CHORUS. When was the first day of your last period?

DESSA. Huh?

HEAD PHYSICIAN. I noticed you're looking off to the side. Are you seeing anything out of the corner of your eye? Spots of light, perhaps?

DESSA. Nothing.

ANGIE. I'll try to not take that personally.

HEAD PHYSICIAN. Are you sure?

DESSA. Yes.

HEAD PHYSICIAN. No fuzziness or blurred vision?

DESSA. No.

HEAD PHYSICIAN. Alright then. We'd like to discuss what you remember from the attack. Can you tell us what happened? Anything you can recall is fine.

DESSA. I was in a convoy heading to the opening of a new, um, where kids...they learn and, you know, where kids go.

ANGIE. School?

DESSA. A school. One we helped build. All I remember is this flash of light, then the sensation of being flung out of the, oh, the um…

ANGIE. Humvee-thing?

HEAD PHYSICIAN. It's ok, anomic aphasia is consistent with this type of injury.

ANGIE. One more time in English?

DESSA. Huh?

HEAD PHYSICIAN. A little forgetfulness is normal. What else do you remember?

DESSA. I remember being…thrown. From the Humvee. That's it. Some flashes of the hospital. Nothing that makes sense until I got here.

CHORUS. We've noticed some discrepancies in your story.

HEAD PHYSICIAN. Do you mind if we ask you about them?

DESSA. What do you mean?

*The beeping heartbeat monitor in the background speeds up and grows loud*er.

DOCTOR 1. You were wearing your safety belt.

DOCTOR 2. Which means ejection was unlikely.

DOCTOR 3. And you were rescued from inside the vehicle.

DESSA, *visibly agitated*. No. I remember flying out.

DOCTOR 4, *aside to* DOCTOR 5. That's the post-traumatic amnesia talking.

DESSA. It's what I remember.

HEAD PHYSICIAN. Captain Daniels, we have the incident report right here. There were photos taken at the scene placing you in the vehicle. It was propelled into the air and flipped over, but you remained inside.

DESSA. I don't understand…

HEAD PHYSICIAN. That's alright. We're here to help you understand. To move forward in your rehabilitation, you sometimes have to go backwards. Work through your memories.

DOCTOR 5. You've been through a lot.

DOCTOR 6. Your memory will return in time.

DOCTOR 7. Except if it doesn't…

DOCTOR 8. Shh!

HEAD PHYSICIAN. For now, get some rest, we'll check in on you tomorrow.

CHORUS OF DOCTORS, *exits*.

DESSA. I don't understand. That's not…what I remember.

ANGIE. Forget them! *Claps her hands over her mouth*. Sorry. Bad choice of words. What I mean is, ignore that chorus line of stuffy bastards. Your memory will come back.

DESSA. But how quickly? Ang, I don't know what's coming next. I need my next role.

ANGIE. Leave that to me. I'll take care of planning your comeback.

DESSA. How can I act again if I can't even remember, ah, what is it?

ANGIE. Words?

DESSA. Words! Words! Words!

The heartbeat monitor in the background beeps more rapidly

ANGIE. You already did that show. That wasn't even your line.

DESSA. I can't remember!

ANGIE. That's fine, honey. No one wants to sit through Hamlet anyway.

DESSA. Forget Hamlet! I can't remember anything! I'm good for nothing. How am I supposed to do a, a…

ANGIE. Comeback?

DESSA, *yells inaudible and sobs. The heartbeat monitor beeps furiously.*

ANGIE. Hey, hey. It's ok. Listen. We don't have to talk about this now. Hey. Remember back when you were on set for "Growing Up?" The day I took you to the Bronx Zoo?

DESSA. That was a fun day. You were cheering me up.

The heartbeat monitor gradually slows.

ANGIE. You needed the break after that awful director screamed at you. He was such a bastard. Started ranting and throwing things because you couldn't remember your lines. When we passed by the condors, remember what you said?

DESSA, *laughing softly.* Yeah. I said the director looked like them.

ANGIE. Right. Because of all the creepy skin on his neck.

DESSA. He didn't like it when I told him that later.

ANGIE. Well, he shouldn't have waited that long for a rhytidectomy. And he shouldn't have bullied you on set, either. You were ten, for god's sake.

DESSA. That's how it was. How it is.

ANGIE. He was a maniac.

DESSA. It's not just him. It's everywhere. You perform or you die.

ANGIE. Easy, Dessa. No performance is that dire.

DESSA, *slurring her words and drifting off to sleep.* The one I just left, that was.

ANGIE. You were in the military, hon. Still are. You put your performing days on hold.

DESSA. No. You're wrong. They call it a theater of operations for a reason.

ANGIE. Still, it's not the same.

DESSA. But it is. You should've seen me, Ang. Briefing Generals, members of the press. Directing a team. Acting confident, even when I was scared. I was…center stage.

ANGIE. I'm sure you were great, honey. You always are.

DESSA. You don't get it. It was real, but it was a show. Everywhere I went, people noticed. Stared. They knew my backstory. I had my role to play. You can't make a mistake in that kind of role. Even the simple stuff, a convoy to a, what was it?

ANGIE. A school.

DESSA. A convoy to a school. Even that was dangerous. It wasn't supposed to be in the script. But it was. And now my part is over.

ANGIE. Want me to leave you for a bit? So, you can get some rest?

DESSA. No, stay with me, Ang. Just a little while longer.

ANGIE. OK, honey. You rest up. I'm here. I'm not going anywhere.

END SCENE

Act II

ORDERLY *enters. Takes away* DESSA's *tray. As he does, he turns to the audience and speaks.*

ORDERLY. Act Two. Telling the story.

CHORUS OF DOCTORS *enters.*

HEAD PHYSICIAN. Alright, team. Update on Captain Daniels.

CHORUS. Patient is demonstrating improvements in her hand-eye coordination. She still struggles with the names of objects and people, exhibits confusion, but the patient is progressing! The patient is progressing!

DOCTOR 1. Her story is inconsistent.

DOCTOR 2. She's in therapy—

DOCTOR 3. But she's resistant.

CHORUS. The patient is progressing!

DOCTOR 4. There's work to be done...

CHORUS. But she's progressing!

DOCTOR 5. Her physical healing is right on track.

DOCTOR 6. But let's not forget...

DOCTOR 7. Only two others survived the attack.

DOCTOR 8. Emotional trauma is improvisational.

DOCTOR 9. An excruciating routine...

DOCTOR 10. But anything is possible.

CHORUS. The patient is progressing!

ANGIE *enters.* These friggin' guys again.

CHORUS. The patient is progressing!

HEAD PHYSICIAN. And what are the three stages of recovery from a psychological trauma?

CHORUS. Establishing safety, telling the story, reconnecting with others.

CHORUS. Wake up, Captain Daniels. We need to take your vitals.

DESSA. Fine.

CHORUS. Do you know what day it is?

DESSA. Tuesday.

CHORUS. Excellent!

HEAD PHYSICIAN. Wait. How'd you know that?

DESSA. It's written behind you on the, um…

CHORUS. What's behind us?

DESSA. The thing with writing.

CHORUS, *scribbling*. Hmmm…

HEAD PHYSICIAN. Your story, Captain Daniels, is an unusual one. Out of curiosity, what made you want to join the Marines?

DESSA. Clearly not the healthcare.

HEAD PHYSICIAN. Let's move on, then. We keep getting stuck on the events leading up to the accident. Can you tell me what you remember from that day?

DESSA. I already told you. We were opening a school nearby. Some of the guys provided security all throughout the, um, building of it.

ANGIE. Construction.

DESSA. Yes, construction. I went in the convoy with one of the journalists hanging around our unit, covering the war.

CHORUS. She's still looking off to the side. What should we make of that?

HEAD PHYSICIAN. Did you normally accompany squadrons on patrol?

DESSA. No. This was a public event. I was the public affairs officer. It made sense for me to go.

CHORUS. What happened next?

DESSA. The convoy was attacked. An IED or something. I don't know. All I remember is a flash and the feeling of flight, of being ejected from the car.

HEAD PHYSICIAN. From the car?

DESSA. From the Humvee.

HEAD PHYSICIAN. Captain, you were found in the vehicle.

DESSA. Then why do I have this memory?

HEAD PHYSICIAN. Sometimes the mind implants false memories. It's a defense mechanism the brain adopts to attempt to piece together a story.

DESSA. But I can remember, right? If I keep trying?

CHORUS. Maybe. Or maybe not.

DESSA. Great…

HEAD PHYSICIAN. The best thing you can do is try to be patient with the healing process.

DESSA. What about the others in the convoy? Paula especially. How is she doing?

HEAD PHYSICIAN. Are you talking about Paula Peters? Was she in the convoy with you?

DESSA. Yes.

HEAD PHYSICIAN. We don't have the details about everyone in the convoy, but Paula—it's been over the news. She didn't survive her injuries. I'm sorry to have to tell you.

DESSA. She didn't?

HEAD PHYSICIAN. This must come as a shock. We can bring in a grief counselor.

DESSA, *visibly shaken.* Not today. I want to…I'm tired. Thanks for telling me.

HEAD PHYSICIAN. You're lucky to be alive, you know.

DESSA. Lucky. Right.

HEAD PHYSICIAN. Alright then. We'll check in on you later.

CHORUS. Onward! Onward with rounds!

Exit CHORUS of DOCTORS.

ANGIE. Honey. Are you alright?

DESSA. Yes. No. I mean, what did I expect. It was a bad attack. I just thought…hoped…Paula would be okay. I liked her, is all.

ANGIE. Who is this Paula person?

DESSA. Paula Peters. She was a journalist. She was embedded with our battalion to cover the war.

ANGIE. Oof. Journalists are like sports cars, honey. They make you look good but can get you into an awful wreck.

DESSA. She was one of the good ones. Well-known. Respected. I liked her. Spoke with her a lot. She…she knew my story, Ang. Was going to write an article about me.

ANGIE, *growing increasingly animated as she speaks.* She was? Does this mean…does this mean you wanted a comeback, even before the accident?

DESSA. Possibly. Honestly, I didn't know what I expected. But it was my third deployment in five years. I was tired. I wanted my next role.

ANGIE. And now?

DESSA. All that's gone now.

ANGIE. It doesn't have to be.

DESSA. Ang, I went out on that convoy because Paula would be there. To show off or something, I don't know. I strayed from the script. Look where it landed me.

ANGIE, *to the audience.* I could never, for the life of me, figure out how Dessa made the leap from show business to the military. Pursuing theater? Understandable. After her mother passed, she needed something different. But the Marines, of all branches? For years, I thought this was some sort of asceticism thing. Nothing keeps you clean like five a.m. wake ups and mandatory drug tests. [ANGIE *pauses, sighs.*]

    Dessa's mom died in a car accident. Overdosed while behind the wheel. Dessa was with her, too, right there in the passenger's seat. She spent weeks in the hospital, but still, it's a miracle she survived. Once she was out of the hospital, though, Dessa started dipping her fingers into her mom's old stash. Look, I grew up in New York in the seventies. I fault no one for a little casual usage. That's not what this was. Dessa was actively trying to destroy herself. One day, after a particularly bad trip, I found Dessa—Staten Island, of all God-forsaken all places! Holed up in a basement apartment with some cretin with a pierced lip. Lying on a bare mattress after taking God-knows-what. I told her—

ANGIE and DESSA, *in unison.* Get up, honey.

ANGIE. This isn't your part. The pool of washed-up child actors is saturated.

ANGIE and DESSA, *in unison.* Get up, honey. Right now.

ANGIE, *to the audience.* And she got up. I thought she'd be safe after that.

DESSA, *to the audience.* After college, I volunteered with this nonprofit that offered acting lessons to veterans. It's cathartic, really, expressing your own emotions through another persona. That was the point of the program and the veterans I worked with thought so, too. What surprised me, though, is how almost every one of them wanted to go back. The Army or the Marine Corps might have been done with them, but they still longed for the camaraderie of it all. The excitement. They were scarred and missing limbs, and couldn't sleep through the night without screaming, but they still missed it. They wanted that sense of purpose back. Their role defined them. I wanted that. I had lost all sense of who I was at that point. I didn't realize then that some roles can't be reprised.

ANGIE, *to the audience.* I thought Dessa would be safe for a while. She was doing well, in school, volunteering, acting. I thought she was done trying to destroy herself.

DESSA, *to the audience.* After working with the veteran's group for a while, I couldn't help but think, we're not so different, really. We're both playing a part designed to change how people view the world. We've both seen our share of tragedy, know a little something about the price you pay for a performance falling short. Except they actually changed things; all I could do, even at my best, was help the audience escape for a while. It sounds crazy, but I went to a recruiter's office and signed up for Officer Candidate School.

DESSA, *back in the hospital bed.* You know, I wore shoes that were two sizes too small the entire time we filmed "The Secret Door." All eleven months.

ANGIE. Why didn't you say something?

DESSA. Wardrobe gave me the wrong size. I must have grown from the screen test to the start of production. I remember thinking, well, my character is younger than I am, so her shoes must be smaller. I wasn't in my body, anyway. I was in my character's. And as long as I could escape into her skin, I no longer felt my toes curling under the soles of my feet. I think they were broken at one point.

ANGIE. Why did you insist on doing this to yourself?

DESSA, *shrugging*. That's how it was. Even at twelve. You had to destroy a little of yourself if you were going to make something beautiful.

ANGIE. That's not true. An actor's power only increases with usage. Anton Chekhov said that.

DESSA. Michael Chekhov.

ANGIE. At my age, be impressed that I remember anyone's name.

DESSA. And that's a terrible paraphrase.

ANGIE. That's beside the point. You don't need to tear yourself up to perform.

DESSA. Yeah, well, maybe I do. Honestly, I wanted to. It was the only way I could escape.

ANGIE. Escape what? Your mother?

CHORUS OF DOCTORS, *enters*.

ANGIE. Oh, good, the brain trust returns. Twice in one day.

CHORUS. We're here with an update.

DESSA. What's wrong? Was it my scans?

HEAD PHYSICIAN. No, just some administration. Due to the severity of your injuries, the Marine Corps is going to expedite the processing of your medical retirement.

DESSA. What?

HEAD PHYSICIAN. You're still entitled to the same care, and you'll continue to receive retirement pay. We'll send a benefits rep in to talk to you about it.

DESSA. But why?

HEAD PHYSICIAN. Being treated as a military retiree opens more options for you once you depart the hospital. This is for the best.

DESSA. What does this mean? They can't do that. They can't just throw me out.

The heartbeat monitor beeps more rapidly.

ANGIE. Honey, this just speeds up your comeback. You were going to get out anyway.

DESSA. But what am I now? I don't have my next role yet. What will be my next role?

The heartbeat monitor beeps frantically. The doctors rush to her side.

DOCTOR 1. Her blood pressure is rising.

DOCTOR 2. She risks stroking with her head injuries.

ANGIE. Dessa, do you hear them? Take a deep breath, honey.

DESSA *starts convulsing.* No! They can't do this! They can't do this, Angie!

DOCTOR 3. Who's Angie?

DOCTOR 4. Is she hallucinating?

HEAD PHYSICIAN. Dessa? Dessa, who are you talking to?

ANGIE, *shrieking.* Dessa, please!

DOCTOR 5. Call for sedation.

DOCTOR 6. Activate stroke protocols as a precaution.

DESSA. But I don't have my next role yet! Angie, I don't have my role!

END SCENE

Act III

PHYSICAL THERAPIST *enters. He proceeds to fleet and extend her arm.* DESSA *winces in pain with each motion. He counts the repetitions, tells her she's doing a good job, comments on her progress. He then hands* DESSA *different objects- a spoon, a pen, a tennis ball. She grabs at each one, missing the first two times, grabbing it on the third.* PHYSICAL THERAPIST *directs her limbs toward the object and manipulates her hand around it.* DESSA *grunts, strains, then drops it.* PHYSICAL THERAPIST *tells her she's coming along nicely, to keep at it. Says he'll be back with a heating pad. He exits the room, but as he does, he stops and turns to the audience.*

PHYSICAL THERAPIST. Act three. Reconnecting.

ANGIE *enters, addresses the audience.* You've probably figured out by now that I don't exist. Not in the physical sense. See, the living, breathing Angie Fangonella retired when Dessa's prospects started drying up in her teenage years. But me? I stuck with her. I'll always be there when she needs me.

CHORUS OF DOCTORS enters.

HEAD PHYSICIAN. When people are faced with traumatic experiences, they primarily focus on survival and self-protection. They experience a mixture of:

DOCTOR 1. Withdrawal.

DOCTOR 2. Confusion.

DOCTOR 3. Shock.

DOCTOR 4. Some patients try to take action.

DOCTOR 5. Others dissociate.

DOCTOR 6. When a precipitating event is the result of an attack by a family member...

DOCTOR 7. Or a trusted institution...

DOCTOR 8. Patients are prone to increased dependence.

DOCTOR 9. This makes them vulnerable to emotion-focused coping...

DOCTOR 10. Where the patient alters her emotional state...

DOCTOR 1. Or creates a fantasy to escape into...

DOCTOR 2. Rather than confront the circumstances that give rise to those emotional states.

HEAD PHYSICIAN. These factors increase the likeliness of a PTSD diagnosis, characterized by repeated reliving of memories of the traumatic experience that keep drawing the patient back.

CHORUS. Back, back, backwards. They keep drawing the patient back. (*Exits*)

ANGIE. Have you eaten anything?

DESSA. How? I can't even hold a spoon.

ANGIE. Ring for the corpsman.

DESSA. Not hungry.

ANGIE. Honey, you'll never heal if you don't eat something.

DESSA. Stop antagonizing me!

She screams and flings her finger monitor at ANGIE. *The beeping of the monitor stops.*

ANGIE. Nice work on your verbal progress, honey, but ouch. I'm only trying to help.

DESSA. With what? You heard the doctors. I should have died with the others in that convoy.

ANGIE. How could you say that? Don't you dare say that! Besides, you said it yourself. You wanted to get out.

DESSA. Get out on my own terms. With my next role lined up. Not kicked out without my approval! Why do I keep losing, Angie?

ANGIE. What do you mean?

DESSA. Paula was my way to get my story out there. Now she's gone. I aged out of the industry, too old for the precocious child roles, not sexy enough for the leading lady. Theater worked for a while, but people resented me in that world.

ANGIE. Oh, to hell with them. The military probably paid better than the theater, anyway.

DESSA. I loved it, you know. The thrill of live performance. But I was seen as a washed-up movie star taking roles from dedicated dramatists. It's why I took my bow and moved on. To something real.

ANGIE. What about your comeback?

DESSA. Really, Ang? Am I supposed to perform like this? After a ten-year hiatus?

ANGIE. That's the point of a comeback.

DESSA. Right. The comeback created by my imaginary manager. I can barely remember my name most days, never mind the details of the attack that landed me here. But go ahead, send me out for auditions! There's nothing left for me, Angie.

ANGIE. You said this to me once before, you know.

DESSA. I doubt it.

ANGIE. After the car crash. You were in the hospital then, too. Do you remember what happened that night?

DESSA. No.

ANGIE. Don't be a nudge. Think.

DESSA. I was, what, sixteen? My mom had taken me to another audition, and I absolutely bombed it. It was for some television show featuring a bunch of high schoolers and I…I couldn't find a way to slip into my role. How could I; I hadn't set foot in a school since kindergarten.

ANGIE. Good. How did you get to the audition?

DESSA. My mom. She drove me, which was weird.

ANGIE. Why was that weird?

DESSA. She was driving in the city.

ANGIE. Ugh. The price of parking alone.

DESSA. She insisted. Said she wanted to hype me up for it. She only made me nervous, and I rarely ever got nervous. I'd already lost five or six other roles in a row before that, and I choked on that one, too. I couldn't perform the way I should. Anyway, she got high in the car waiting for me. Was in no shape to drive when I got back from the audition. I went with her anyway.

ANGIE. Dessa, what do you remember from the accident?

DESSA. Not much. More of what came before it. Mom yelling, driving too fast, swerving, me yelling back at her, telling her I was going to jump out. I was going to do it, too. Then she veered off to the left. I felt…the impact of it all. It seemed like an explosion we hit so hard. And then… oh God…

ANGIE. Then what? Dessa, tell me.

DESSA, *crying.* I couldn't perform, Angie. It cost me my future. It cost me my mom's life.

ANGIE. You didn't cause any of this. Your mom was high. The convoy was attacked.

DESSA. I don't have a role. Again.

ANGIE. Think about it—this is the second time you've survived something you shouldn't have. It's miraculous.

DESSA. What good's a miracle when you have nothing?

ANGIE. You have everything! Everything can only come from nothing. Remember when I pulled you out of that hovel in Staten Island? Think of all you accomplished after that. You reinvented yourself.

DESSA. I had your help.

ANGIE. No, honey. You invented me. It's time for you to take credit for your own productions.

DESSA *shifts abruptly in her bed.* Oh, God. Oh, God, Ang.

ANGIE. Honey, what is it.

DESSA. I remember. You said it yourself; this was the second time I survived something I shouldn't have.

ANGIE. What are you saying?

DESSA. The first crash.

ANGIE. You're going back—

DESSA. Because you must go back to go forward.

ANGIE *kisses the top of* DESSA's *head.* Dessa, I'm...

CHORUS OF DOCTORS, *enters.* Good morning, Dessa! How are you feeling?

ANGIE. Jesus, Mary, and Joseph. Go ahead and interrupt the moment we were having.

DESSA. I'm...sore. Everything hurts.

CHORUS. You know what we're going to ask.

DESSA. I keep telling you. I haven't had my period since before the accident.

CHORUS. The other question.

DESSA, *sighs.* I...I actually think I remember now.

HEAD PHYSICIAN, *grabs* DESSA's *hand.* Go ahead. When you're ready.

DESSA, *breathes in deeply.* It was morning, just as the sun crept over the mountains and the day was already hot and we were all already sweating. I'd strapped myself into the Humvee and was holding on tightly. Afghanistan, America—I always hated being a passenger. It wasn't supposed to be a dangerous convoy. But then the Humvee in front of us was hit. The driver swerved. Then came the secondary explosion.

It felt like we were lifted off the ground. This big, heavy piece of machinery, just lifted like it was nothing. The impact. It made it seem like someone squeezed my chest and all my insides. Suddenly. Violently. The Humvee came down again and flipped somewhere along the way. I could see the rest of them, tossed inside. They looked...

DESSA *starts to shake and get emotional.* I was so, so confused, wondering how this could happen. How a person could be sitting there one moment, and then the next moment they're.... There was no pain just then. But there was awareness. Awareness and confusion. The last thing I remember going through my mind, "I'm here. I'm here. I'm still here."

HEAD PHYSICIAN. Thank you for sharing this with us, Dessa. It must have been harrowing.

DESSA. Yeah.

HEAD PHYSICIAN. Where do you think the other story came from?

DESSA. I was in a car crash as a teenager. I kept mixing the two together.

HEAD PHYSICIAN. Traumatic events like this will always try to draw you back in time.

CHORUS. Back, back, back.

HEAD PHYSICIAN. That's paradox of treatment. The only way to move on is first to go back.

CHORUS. Without getting stuck in the past.

HEAD PHYSICIAN. Our task is to help you consider the future. To create your new reality and move ahead with it.

CHORUS. Onward!

DESSA. Creation always takes its toll.

HEAD PHYSICIAN. Not necessarily. Even when the mind is insistent on destruction, the body usually trends toward healing.

DESSA. So, the idea is to get them both to sync up?

HEAD PHYSICIAN. Exactly. You've made excellent progress, Dessa. We'll leave you now to rest.

DESSA. Thanks.

CHORUS OF DOCTORS *scatters. The unified chorus dissolves. Their tight formation loosens to a more natural presence. Some exit stage left, others stage right. As they weave their way through the room, differences start to appear. Some sling their stethoscopes down their backs, others tuck them in their pockets. Doctors depart from the room and return with their hair in a ponytail or wearing a turban. Glasses are removed or replaced. They become fully formed individuals going about their tasks separately.* HEAD PHYSICIAN *makes notes on a digital chart, hands it off to another physician, points and directs corpsmen to attend to* DESSA's *IV bags. One by one, each physician exits the room. Overhead, spotlights directed at* DESSA *dim. She's left alone under the buzzing fluorescent bulbs, no longer on stage, but in a brightly lit room crowded with machines. The sound of conversations echoing down the hallway and squeaky gurneys drift into the room, then subside.*

ANGIE. That's the first bit of sense I've heard them speak in weeks.

DESSA. It's easy for them to talk about moving ahead. I'll bet their lives are predictable.

ANGIE. Where's the fun in that?

DESSA. I suppose.

ANGIE. All this has me thinking. Honey, I think it may be time.

DESSA. Time for what?

ANGIE. Well, you heard them. You took a big step today, reconciling the past and all that. But you can't keep looking backwards.

DESSA. Look, if this is about the comeback, I'll give it some more thought.

ANGIE. I hope you do. But…you'll have to do it without me.

DESSA. What are you saying?

ANGIE. I'm saying that it's time you focus on yourself. In real time. No
made-up plays or characters to escape into.

DESSA. Angie, no. No way. I'm not ready.

ANGIE. Yes, you are. Consider this your third act. That's always the best part
of the show.

DESSA. Please, Ang. I don't know what I'm doing.

ANGIE. Just know I'm so, so proud of you.

DESSA. Please, don't. I can't do this without you.

*

But there's no one in the room. Just me, alone with the beeping monitors, the
soundtrack to my heartbeat and breathing. Recalling me to the body dangling in slings and encased in casts. Reminders of the characters I've created
to escape my own body.

Please, please, you can't. Don't go, I say.

Angie doesn't answer me. No one does. There's no one left. I've survived
them all.

I don't want the pain of a disengaged mind, forced to focus on the itch
and pull of my sutures, the constant throbbing in my skull so powerful it feels
as if it will split through my skin. The heat and tingle of my dormant limbs,
dead weight aflame. The stabbing sensation at my hips and lower back. The
ever-present acidic surge of my stomach, an antibiotic-induced gurgle. My
flesh cracking in the arid hospital air—split lips and heels, a coat of white,
flaking skin covering each limb. I hit the call button, then the pump to increase the Tramadol dose. No relief arrives. I strike it again and again.

There's nothing but this, as far as I can tell. Months and months of
skull-pulsing, ligament pulling adjustment. Of learning to walk and feed and
speak for myself. No other role or body to fold myself into. Just Dessa. And
figuring out who she is.

The next script is blank, waiting to be written. Nothing follows it unless
I create it for myself. Every part I've played demanded directorial oblation,
a sacrifice of myself to fulfill someone else's vision or mission. What will I
demand of myself? Healing is the only thing which comes to mind. A performance insistent on repair.

The rest of the script will come in time. For now, the opening lines are
already starting to form: *I am here, I am here, I am still here.*

DEAD BABY JOKES

Despite the calm surface, the Gulf of Aden exhaled and inhaled in large swells. Our target, a blue and white fishing dhow, seemed to disappear against the cerulean backdrop of the clear afternoon sky. Five silhouettes scurried across the deck, tossing objects over the side as they ran. The harsh glare of the sun effaced their finer features, reducing the dhow's crew to shadows shifting against a blinding backdrop. One short and burly. Three tall and lanky. One figure looked much smaller than the others.

Overhead, the SH-60 assigned to our ship circled the dhow, spreading ripples across the water's surface. The air crew issued verbal commands from a megaphone like a wrathful god: *You have been identified by the United States Navy as a vessel of interest. Slow your speed and prepare to be boarded for inspection.*

"Stay alert, gents. We're not boarding if it looks too hot," I directed over the net. Crammed next to the eleven other members of my team on our small boat, the swirling under-currents and the pungent odor of exhaust emitted by the boat's diesel engine nauseated me.

"Come on, ma'am. We haven't shot up one of these boats all deployment," Edwards replied, his Louisiana drawl dragging lazily over the radio.

"Think we can sink this one, ma'am?" Tyler said. "Bet it'd burn like a mother with that wooden hull."

I smirked involuntarily, then pinched the inside of my forearm until a welt emerged.

"We're not shooting up dhows for the hell of it," I said. As I looked through my binoculars, I watched as the tiny figure sprinted across the deck. I lost sight of him, regained it, then lost him again as the rhib bucked in the rotor wash. "Besides, it looks like there's a kid onboard."

We hadn't seen children during any of our previous searches. Surly teenagers, sure, though the harsh living conditions in the Horn of Africa made all inhabitants appear much older than they actually were. It seemed as if childhood ceased to exist in this corner of the world.

"Hey, you need fewer bullets for kids," Tyler said. "Know the difference between a truck fulla bricks and a truck fulla dead babies, ma'am?"

"Cut it out, Tyler," I said.

"You don't have to unload bricks with a pitchfork."

"Those aren't funny," I replied.

Despite my admonition, several helmeted heads bounced up and down. You'd think they'd be less eager to laugh. Two of the guys' wives gave birth since we left on deployment. Three others had little ones on the way. A phantom cramp caused me to curl forward slightly.

"Actually, ma'am, people can't help but laugh 'bout terrible things," Edwards said. "It's an emotional defense. Your brain can't make sense of the pieces."

"Oh good," I said. "We've got a bayou philosopher onboard."

"Lighten up, Princess. Dead baby jokes are hilarious," Harrison said over the net. He led our second boarding team, the "support squad"—a moniker he openly loathed. Their rhib trailed several yards behind ours. "Know the only thing funnier than a dead baby?"

"Silence on the net," I ordered. "You all need to get your heads on straight for this boarding."

"A dead baby in a clown costume," Harrison said. He stood and gave me an exaggerated wave. I raised my hand in reply, middle finger extended.

"'Silence on the net' applies to you, too, Harrison," I said. Turning to Chief Jimenez, our team's Senior Enlisted, I asked, "Did your teams act this way when you were in Iraq?"

"Worse," Chief responded. Unlike other members of the boarding team, Chief served a tour on the ground with Army security forces. He returned from the individual augmentation with a Bronze Star and a seemingly endless collection of stories. "I could barely believe the trash that flew outta their mouths. But they saw some real serious shit out there. The worse it got, the more they needed to let loose. All's this team does is act mean in front of a bunch of Somali fishermen."

"We all have our ways of coping," I said, looking away.

Mine had been luring men I met at beachside bars to the back of my car before deployment. The ones I chose had no clue what I did during the day, all the responsibilities I carried. Hell, most never knew my real name. Not that they cared. That's the beauty of being stationed in north Florida. You're surrounded by sweet, stupid Southern boys who will chivalrously open your car door for you, then leave cum stains on your back seat five minutes later.

It made it all the more delicious to kick them out before they could zip their jeans back up. Watching their smiles fade felt more satisfying than the act itself. They never realized they were disposable. Bit players in a pantomime of affection I could pursue without being consumed.

In the morning, I'd return to being the alert and chaste and valiant Lieutenant Bloom, who scales the sides of ships and speaks to kids at local schools about the ways the Navy is saving the world, donning the relentless weight of perfection every time she puts on her uniform. The nocturnal woman existed as a separate self, one unsheathed whenever that weight became too heavy to bear.

"Kali's in a mood," Harrison said in a sing-song cadence. My hands itched with the impulse to clamp around his stumpy neck. I pinched the inside of my forearm again.

"Lock it up, ladies. Lieutenant Bloom said silence on the net," Chief bellowed. My eardrums fluttered in the aftermath of his outburst.

"Five minutes until we come alongside," I said, returning my gaze to the small figure on the dhow bobbing up and down in my field of vision.

Most people—friends, teachers, my own parents—thought the concept of me joining the military was outrageous. They never doubted my talk about service and tradition and a desire to travel. But wouldn't a nice, pretty girl such as myself prefer to do a semester abroad or Teach for America instead?

These people discounted the elbows I threw at the starting line of cross-country races as adolescent volatility. Whenever I tripped rude strangers in crowded bars or stomped on the sandaled feet of men who tried to jump in line before me at concerts, they appeared surprised or laughed as they exclaimed, *I can't believe you just did that!*

No one knew how liberated I felt in those moments. Nor would they ever. The revelation would only repulse them. How could anyone comprehend this urge compelling me to rip the world apart and weave together a new one from the frayed edges? Yet these urges didn't control me; I controlled them. Kali is the referee who keeps them separated, assigning each self to her assigned space. The possibility of their convergence terrified me.

*

Each crew member completed his pre-boarding ritual. Edwards lowered his head, folded his hands, and mouthed a quick prayer. Tyler and Nguyen bumped their fists together in a choreographed pattern. Salim bowed at the waist then lifted his hands toward the sky. Frederick tapped each side of his helmet twice, first with his left hand, again with his right. Chief kissed the medal of Our Lady of Guadalupe he wore around his neck, then tucked it back under his vest.

I had no ritual—I was quick and strong and smart. Why would I believe in anything but myself?

"Boat one, at the ready," I said over the net. "I need everyone to be alert. We've been lucky with our past boardings. Doesn't mean this one will be easy. Salim, with me."

Our helmsman maneuvered the rhib to parallel the dhow's course and slowed to a near idle. Salim, our interpreter, proceeded to join me at the front of the rhib, using each team member's hand as a guard rail to aid his transit forward. I lifted the rhib's hand-held bridge-to-bridge radio to notify the dhow's crew of our intent to board, then passed the radio to Salim, who translated my orders into Somali.

"The bastards probably threw everything overboard by now," Tyler said.

"Let Salim look at any paperwork you find," Chief replied. "Just because you can't read it doesn't mean it doesn't matter."

"That's real mean, Chief," Tyler said. "Since we all know Edwards can't read."

"Now that ain't true, Ty," Edwards replied. "Your mom always writes notes when she sends me pictures of her titties."

The two exchanged playful punches until Chief hollered at them to stop.

"I'm headed up," I said. A few catcalls echoed from below as I climbed out of the rhib.

As team leader, I always boarded first, my every handhold and footfall on full display. The ascent presented a physical challenge as I had to hoist myself into the air while being weighed down by tactical gear. Yet the uncertainty and sense of in-betweenness bothered me the most: the departure from the safety of our own rhib to an unknown vessel; a lone figure hovering between churning sea and solid footing.

Near the rope ladder's final rung, a piercing pain shot through my palm as I grasped the dhow's wooden stanchion. My hand involuntarily retracted, and I glimpsed an exposed nail as I swung backwards, like the hinge of a door, and dangled from the ladder with the right side of my body. I hovered for a few seconds, then swung my body weight back toward the dhow. This time, I grasped the stanchion below the exposed hardware and lifted myself onboard.

"You OK, ma'am?" Chief hollered from the rhib below, not bothering to hide the alarm in his voice.

"Fine," I said. Blood bubbled under my glove. "Tell the team to watch out. There are nails on the stanchions."

"Can't lift yourself, Princess?" Harrison said.

"You stay nice and safe back on the support rhib, Harrison," I replied. "We'll call you if we need a water break." My team members allowed their laughter and raucous responses to spill onto the net. Chief hollered for them to quiet down.

*

To watch a boarding team scale the side of a ship is akin to watching a violent ballet. Team members know their steps and maneuver with a heavy-booted grace, one after the other, to their assigned positions. They survey their surroundings, trigger fingers extended, alert to any lurking threats waiting to reveal themselves.

This boarding marked our team's 22nd search in the past five months. We patrolled the Gulf of Aden to identify vessels suspected of piracy, boarded, and inspected the contents of suspicious ships, and detained the crew if we found sufficient evidence of criminal activity onboard. A hybrid mission combining show-of-force and law enforcement operations, executed by clumsy Sailors who trained in their tactics part time. Pirate ships were taking multiple merchant vessels hostage daily, and our boarding team was assigned to one of three coalition warships tasked with deterring these attacks.

If there were pirates out there, though, we never seemed to find them. Most boats we boarded were merely fishing illegally or smuggling supplies into Yemen, typically alcohol or antiquated electronics. Portable CD players were particularly in vogue. Amusingly, we boarded four separate boats containing crates of flashlights with President Obama's face cartoonishly sketched on the handle. American democracy reduced to kitsch. The guys loved finding those—I had to stop them from pocketing a few for themselves.

As we searched these vessels, their crews stared at us in terror and smoldered with anger, watching as we pried open crates and issued menacing commands. Our heavy tactical gear an absurd contrast to their bare feet and stained macawiis. After a while, I stopped making eye contact with the crews. They undoubtedly saw us as interlopers who dented their cargo and delayed their arrival times. Our destruction served no purpose; we created nothing aside from resentment.

Imposing a sense of order in a region marked by chaos seemed appealing at first; I was young and arrogant enough to think it possible. Not so when disorder was the region's governing principle. Crime and violence offered the only means of survival. Piracy provided men with an alternative to joining terrorist groups infringing on Somali territory from the south. This made us the villains for trying to disrupt it.

*

"Try not to break anything, gents," I called over the net. "Not like last time."

"Yes, mom," Tyler replied. "I mean ma'am."

The dhow's crew assembled on the forward weather deck. Their heads swayed back and forth with the vessel's every roll. Edwards and Nguyen stood on either side of the crew, their hands fixed on their weapons, their weapons trained to the deck. Nguyen had offered them cigarettes. Each man accepted these slender white sticks reverentially but refused Nguyen's offer for a light.

"The captain says he and his crew are fishing. They're not pirates," Salim translated. The dhow's captain gestured wildly as he spoke. He wore a gold chain around his neck and sneered at us with missing teeth, pointing to a pile of tattered fishing nets laying on the deck for emphasis.

"My ass they're fishing with that crap," Edwards said. I snapped my fingers at him, and he returned his attention to the dhow's crew.

"What about his papers?" I asked Salim.

"He says he lost them," Salim replied.

"Convenient," I said. Salim nodded.

The three scrawny men standing beside the captain cast their eyes downward. One wore a bright red t-shirt, stained with oil, and ripped under the arms. Another donned a wrinkled green polo shirt. The third wore a black t-shirt that extended well past his knees and a yellow ball cap with a sun-bleached, illegible logo. All of them, like the captain, had tawny, weather-beaten skin. When Salim asked for their names, they gave no reply.

At their feet sat a boy, barefoot and cavernously thin. He had large dark eyes and a small narrow nose. His skin looked smooth despite the rays of the formidable sun and his hair grew from his scalp in unruly clumps. He wore stained khaki shorts and a white t-shirt that billowed around his slight frame. An unsightly white film covered his feet and climbed up his ankles. Unlike the men, he looked directly at Salim and me. The boy seemed curious and devoid of fear. When he realized I was studying him, he smiled bashfully. The only sign of innocence I'd seen in months. He fumbled his fingers around strands of fishing line, weaving them into an intricately braided lanyard. I smiled back at him.

"Ask the boy how old he is," I instructed Salim.

"Sixteen," Salim translated. The captain had provided the reply, not the boy.

As the boy continued to smile at me, I reached into my vest pocket and pulled out a Power Bar I kept in case the boarding ran long. I offered it to him. He accepted it gingerly and cradled it in his hand. I winked at the boy, and he giggled. Then he lifted the lanyard he had been weaving and gestured for me to take it.

"Are you sure?" I asked. The boy smiled and gestured again. He looked dirty and thin and tired, but pure, nonetheless. I accepted the trinket with two hands, thanked him, and tucked it into the pocket of my trousers.

"Bullshit he's sixteen," I said to Salim. "Ask him again." I'd seen intel reports of child trafficking throughout deployment, of horrific conditions for children who, in any other part of the world, were too small to ride a rollercoaster. With his gentle features and slight frame, this kid couldn't be any more than ten.

"Sixteen," Salim translated. Again, the captain provided the reply.

Over the radio, the team made reports as they searched the vessel. I broke away to take a look at what they found. Chief showed me eight rusted fuel barrels strapped to the dhow's stern uprights. He kicked each one for effect. All but two reverberated with a hollow clatter.

"They've burned a lot of oil," he said. "Must've been out here a while."

The smell of rotting fish and unwashed bodies choked me as I climbed a ladder below deck. Objects dangled from the overheads—pots, shirts, tattered headphones. Four hammocks, suspended from the bulkheads, swung as the dhow rolled. I wondered where the boy slept.

Three of the guys huddled over a chart table, chuckling.

"Get a load of this, ma'am," one said, pointing to a stack of at least two dozen porn magazines piled on top of the chart table. "Found these inside a cabinet. Right next to some prayer beads and a rug." Framed by Cyrillic script, the cover models gaped at us from the worn pages as if surprised by our arrival.

"You really want to touch those?" I asked, which caused them to throw the magazines at one another and attempt to rub the pages in each other's faces. This uncovered a stack of nautical charts previously hidden by the porn spread. I instantly recognized the outline of the Gulf of Oman and the Strait of Hormuz.

"What were they doing in the Persian Gulf?" I mused to no one in particular.

"We're not allowed to call it that anymore, ma'am," one of the guys said, clucking his tongue in mock disapproval.

"Enough messing around," I said, and tucked one of the charts into the side of my vest so I could show it to Salim. "Put those back where you got them and look for something useful." As I ascended the ladder to the weather deck, the lanyard shifted in my pocket and pressed against my leg through the fabric.

The boy greeted me with a timid wave. He said something I couldn't understand in a soft, squeaky voice.

"What was that?" I asked. Before the boy could reply, the dhow's captain kicked him between his shoulder blades. He let out a whelp. Then, the boy quickly unwrapped the Power Bar I gave him and stuffed the entire contents into his mouth in a single bite, all while casting the captain a defiant look. I stuck my tongue out in the captain's direction, which made the boy giggle. He spoke again, which made the captain kick him more forcefully than the first time.

"Go easy," I yelled, taking a step toward the captain. The captain muttered something under his breath. I swore back at him. Salim didn't bother to translate.

"Ma'am, a word?" Salim asked. We stepped away from the crew and he lowered his voice to a whisper.

"These men. They're not Somali," Salim said.

"I figured that out just by looking at them," I replied.

"Yes, but the captain is speaking Somali," Salim said. "Badly, but trying to. None of the crew members seem to understand what he says. Then the boy just now, he spoke in Arabic."

"Could you make out his accent?" I asked.

Salim shook his head. "Yemeni, maybe, but who knows. I'd need to hear more."

"Let's keep talking to them," I said. "Especially to the boy. See if he indicates where he's from." I removed the chart from my vest to show Salim, but paused and asked, "What did he say before the captain kicked him?"

Tyler's excited voice broke through the net before Salim could respond.

"Ma'am! Think we found a false deck-plate. We're going to pry it open." The crack of splintering boards followed before I could warn him to be careful.

"Holy shit. Ma'am, come look at this," Frederick called out over the net.

Tyler and Frederick had untethered a large pile of crates previously strapped to the dhow's mast. They knelt between the strewn boxes and propped their weapons against a wooden pallet. Pieces of splintered deckplates lay next to them. Salim's shouts cut through the net before I could see what they had uncovered.

"The captain says to get away from there," Salim said quickly.

"Put it down!" cried Edwards. He didn't bother to key his headset; he yelled loudly enough for us to hear him through our helmets.

"Gun!" Nguyen yelled.

I turned to see Nguyen twisting and shouting as Red Shirt grabbed a hold of his rifle stock and Green Polo pounced on him from behind. Beside them, Edwards scuffled with the captain, grasping for the pistol he brandished in his fleshy hand. A shot resounded, then another in quick succession. Edwards fell.

I gave the order to engage. Out rained death.

The captain fired wildly in the direction of the team, then flailed uncontrollably as his body absorbed the team's return fire. He continued twitching, even after he collapsed to the deck.

I dropped to one knee and took cover before I fired, first at the captain, then at Red Shirt, who had wrenched Nguyen's rifle from him. Two of my rounds hit Red Shirt in the chest, followed by several others from unseen shooters. A confused expression crossed Red Shirt's face as he slunk downward. Dark red blotches blossomed underneath the faded fibers of his shirt. Still, he held onto the rifle and pointed it—weakly—in the team's direction. I took a third shot, but a figure dashed across my scope as I pulled the trigger. By the time I trained my scope on Red Shirt again, he had fallen face-first onto the deck. Yellow Hat lay crumpled in a corner, holding his side and rocking back and forth. Threads of blood oozed between his fingers. I yelled to cease fire three times before the barrage of gunfire stopped. Then the dhow grew still.

One by one, each crew member provided a status report. They emerged cautiously from where they had taken cover, rifles held firmly in front of them. No one trusted this sudden state of calm. Chief interrupted our stunned stupor by sprinting from his position to where Edwards and Nguyen had fallen. I radioed the helicopter crew for a medical evacuation and ordered Harrison's crew to board for assistance. Frederick applied pressure to Salim's wounds with his bare hands. Over the radio, our ship's commanding officer's screams for a status report dulled to a whimpering plea.

"It's about goddamn time!" he shouted when I responded, then followed up with a harried, "Bloom, how's the team? Are you alright?"

Yellow Hat moaned and shook his zip-tied hands at us while one of the guys applied pressure to the wound at his side. Salim leaned against the dhow's superstructure looking dazed. A bullet had grazed the back of his neck on the left side of his body—most likely an errant shot from one of the guys. A shallow wound, though it bled profusely. We evacuated Edwards— pale and half-unconscious but breathing—along with Yellow Hat when the first air lift arrived.

"You're going to make it," I whispered to Edwards as they strapped him to the litter. "Hang in there, okay? We need our bayou philosopher."

The flurry of activity died down around us. Nguyen had a concussion and broken arm. He sat next to Salim awaiting the second airlift. The dhow's Captain, Red Shirt, and Green Polo all lay dead on the deck. They would be removed from the dhow on the third airlift.

"Where's the boy?" I asked. Of the dhow's crew and the boarding team, all but one could be accounted for. "Has anyone seen the boy?"

"He went overboard during the shooting, ma'am," Frederick said. "Port side."

By the time I reached the side of the dhow, all I could see was a parting glimpse of a dark mass—the boy's body sinking below the surface. Rising swells of blood spiraled up from his wounds, obscuring his delicate facial features. Chief and Harrison stepped beside me.

"Send the other rhib over," I said. "We don't know how badly he's been wounded."

"He's too deep, ma'am," Chief responded softly. "Too far gone."

"He's only a kid, Chief," I said, removing my hands from the dhow's stanchions. Blood from the cut on my hand had seeped through my glove. It left a red smudge on the weathered wooden surface. "We can at least recover his body."

"There's no point in doing that now, Princess," Harrison said. "Bricks and dead babies. They both sink."

*

No one spoke on the rhib as we returned to the ship. I twisted the boy's lanyard in my right hand while I cradled my left hand in my lap. The wound felt tight and hot and pulsated underneath the newly applied bandage.

"I'm sorry," I whispered, words consumed by the din of the boat's engine.

Despite the heat, I couldn't stop trembling. A memory drifted in, unbidden and unwelcome. The doctor's office before deployment. I shivered then, too, in my paper gown. The one I left bloodied after the procedure. I apologized to one of the technicians about it, when really, I was apologizing to myself. Not for the loss—all I felt was relief and a little cramping—but for my carelessness. Discretion was the price of entry for this profession; there could only be perfection or the pain of falling short. It didn't matter if I vivisected myself into separate pieces daily, the knife could never slip. Sometimes I wonder if to be a woman is to bleed and apologize for it.

"You shouldn't hold on to that," Chief said, pointing at the lanyard. "Throw it overboard." I closed my fist around it.

The loss of the dhow's crew caused me no guilt. I expected some reaction to their deaths. None came. They had to be eliminated for something new to grow. Like the boy.

"Why the fuck didn't the kid take cover?" I yelled out without warning, slamming my bandaged left hand against the hull. Pain jolted through my palm. The remaining team members in the rhib shifted uncomfortably.

"These things happen, ma'am," Chief said. "You can't control everything."

*

Back on our ship, the crew reported to the armory to take off their gear and provide their statements, while Chief and I proceeded to the commanding officer's stateroom to debrief him.

"I gave the order to engage," I said, slumping in my chair and gripping the armrest with my right hand to keep myself from collapsing even further. "The dhow's captain and two crew members were hit multiple times. Another sustained minor injuries. The boy—"

"The fourth crew member," the commanding officer interrupted.

"The fourth crew member jumped up and ran. He must have been caught in the crossfire and propelled over the side." *A figure darting across my rifle scope.* "Tyler and Frederick found a cache of weapons hidden under a false deck-plate right before the captain attacked. Mostly AKs and boxes of Chinese ammo. Four RPGs that had seen better days. We suspect this is what set him off. Whoever he was working for apparently posed more of a threat than we did."

"Good," the commanding officer said. He asked a few questions, then made me tell and retell the story until the words passing from my mouth felt as smooth and cold as the metal casing of a bullet.

"We'll get through this," Chief Jiménez said as we exited the commanding officer's stateroom. "You know I'll always have your back." He suffocated me with the weight of his bear-like arm around my shoulder.

Harrison awaited us when we arrived at the armory. I tried to remove my gear without looking at him but couldn't avoid seeing his reflection appear in the mirror bolted to a bulkhead at the furthest end of the compartment. A mirthless smile spread across his face.

"You know, Princess, I knew this day would come. I told the CO before deployment that I should've been in charge. Now you've probably gotten Edwards killed," Harrison said. Then, raising his voice to a yell, he added, "Who doesn't check to see if the crew is armed?"

"Lieutenant Bloom checked. I checked," Chief said. He thrust his chest in Harrison's direction. "You some kind of psychic who knew they'd pull weapons out their ass?"

"Give it a rest, Chief," Harrison said. "No need to go down with her."

"Shut your mouth, sir," Chief hissed. "I'm not going to tell you again."

"Know what, Chief, my bad. I should be congratulating Kali on her kills," Harrison said. He spoke without turning away from Chief. Daring him to make a move. "How about it, Princess? How do you feel about dead baby jokes now?"

Both were too preoccupied to see me spring forward and grasp Harrison's neck.

Harrison stumbled backwards from the force of my forward momentum, tripping over his own feet and veering backwards. I maintained my grip on his neck, squeezing with all my might, and fell with Harrison, raising my knees and striking them against his ribcage as we landed. His head hit the deck with a sickening crack. Harrison's eyes bulged from his head, and he rolled frantically from side to side, emitting guttural chokes and striking at me in vain. Spittle flew from his gaping mouth and dribbled onto my hands. I maintained my grip.

A strange thought possessed me as the force of his flailing grew weaker: once his neck broke, so too would some division inside. These separate selves, kept apart for too long, would merge then emerge as some new being. Something whole.

Chief's voice sounded muffled and distant. He shook me until my grip loosened and flung me halfway across the armory.

"Walk away, ma'am," he yelled.

My bandage had unraveled. I wound it back around my hand and surveyed Harrison as he lay on the ground, gasping and wheezing. A streak of bright red blood marked his neck.

"Leave your gear and go," Chief said. He didn't look at me as he spoke. "I'll get Lieutenant Harrison back to his room."

"Thank you, Chief," I replied in a dainty voice which sounded as if it came from someone else's mouth.

The boy's lanyard lay next to me on the deck, probably expelled from my pocket during the tussle with Harrison. I picked it up and surveyed it closely; a few lines had frayed, causing the braids to unravel at the ends. Then, for reasons unknown even to myself, I threw my head back and laughed. Chief stared at me, visibly horrified. I didn't care. Nor could I stop, even as tears ran down my face and my diaphragm ached.

I pulled myself to my feet and stumbled to the mirror bolted at the back of the armory, convinced I'd see myself transformed into some savage creature, that other being delivered into this world. I saw only Kali—hair matted, face covered in salt spray, a sunburnt nose and chin—   but otherwise unchanged. The same person I'd always been.

THE PATRON SAINT OF CRUISE MISSILES

The call comes like all supernatural invocations do—in the dark, unannounced. Shaken by the scream of the stateroom's telephone, I sit upright, feeling the acid wash of panic accompanying the sudden jolt from slumber. One roommate flips restlessly in the bunk underneath mine, the other snores softly in the rack above. I grab the phone and Blaine's voice fills my ears.

"Kira, I need you," he says. My heartbeat pounds in my ears, tempered only when he adds, "Come down to Combat now." Blaine never asks me for anything. He demands I sit beside him, walk with him, speak with him, call him by his first name.

"What is it?" I ask.

"We've received strike tasking."

"I'll be right there," I say, and shake off the residue of slumber coating my face and limbs, spin my still-damp hair into a low bun. Purify myself for the ritual ahead.

Our ship has been out to sea for five months. Two months of deployment remain. I won't mention where we are. It doesn't matter. U.S. ships are launching missiles into three different countries and we're hundreds of miles away each time.

Red lights flood my vision when I stumble into Combat. Blaine sits sideways in the tactical action officer's chair, facing the doorway, and leaps from his seat—too eagerly— as I enter. In his hand, he holds a red-rimmed folder labeled with insistent classification markers.

"What happened?" I ask.

"Suicide bomber at a voting center," he replies. "Killed seventeen Marines and at least thirty locals. A lot more were injured, so that number's going to go up."

A churn of dread and rage ignites in my stomach. I'm never without this sensation for long. The burn of absence. The fury that accompanies loss. The news only amplifies this feeling—my body tenses and trembles.

"Mother of God," I say, the rote responses of my youth to taking over.

"I love it when your inner Catholic school girl emerges," Blaine says.

"Not now," I whisper.

"The retaliatory strike launches in another few hours," he replies, and hands me the folder. My hand shakes as I grab it. I know what lies inside.

"Kira, get yourself together," Blaine says. "You need to be ready for this."

"I've been ready," I say. "For too long."

Blaine nods. "Good. Let's call the captain."

Inside the folder is a copy of the cruise missile checklist, our gospel and our missal, the litany of activities performed to bring about the ruin of an un-suspecting target. The command *Notify the commanding officer of tasking* appears at the top of the cruise missile checklist. We're in the preparatory stages now. Things will move slowly at first. There's no magic button which sends a missile careening hundreds of miles away on a whim. No spontaneous light-ning strike from a vengeful god. It's a slow, protracted roll of thunder.

The captain picks up the phone on the seventh ring.

"What," he grumbles into the receiver.

"Sir, it's Strike. The TAO and I need you down in Combat," I say. We're all known by abbreviated versions of our job titles, not our actual names. It strips you of all sense of identity aside from your most immediate function onboard.

"For what?" The captain's voice sounds raspy and weak.

"Sir, we received a launch package."

"An exercise at this hour?"

"This is real-world tasking, sir. We're launching missiles in eleven hours."

On the other end of the receiver, I hear rustling sheets, creaking bed springs, and a sharp inhalation of breath.

"Lord have mercy," the captain says. "Real-world tasking? Oh, Christ have mercy. I'll be right down."

The captain arrives in Combat a half-hour later, smelling faintly of shaving cream. Water droplets christen the base of his closely buzzed hair. The strike team assembled in combat prior to his arrival, bleary-eyed and sleep-rumpled, smelling like sweat and fermenting breath.

"That vain prick showered before he came down here, didn't he?" Chief Bishop whispers. As the strike divisional chief, she stands with the rest of the yawning strike team.

"This is the moment we've trained for," the captain says. My team members start at the volume of his voice. "Only a few crews are fortunate enough to say they've emptied their magazines into the hearts of the enemy."

"Does he think he's General Fucking Patton?" Chief Bishop whispers. Blaine shushes her.

"In a few hours, we will be entrusted with this sacred duty," the captain continues. "A historic strike into enemy territory."

"We've been doing this shit on repeat for five years," Chief mutters. "They'll be replacing us with drones in a minute."

Blaine shushes her again. She clears her throat.

"Something to say, Chief?" the captain asks.

"Sir, we're on a deadline for processing the launch tasking," Chief says as quietly as possible. But nothing about Chief Bishop is quiet. She stands a head taller than most men on the ship. Her prominent bust and vicious scowl announce her arrival long before she opens her mouth. Being around Chief makes me feel bolder, more daring. "Strike needs to get your approval to start planning in the next few minutes."

"You should have said so," the captain replies. "Go ahead, Strike."

I exhale a shaky breath. When practicing the strike reports during exercises, the words would always fall to the deck as passionless syllables. Now, their weight feels like a leaden communion wafer on my tongue.

"Sir, we've received a launch order, salvo size of thirty-three. Strike team is on station. The bridge team has been briefed and is currently in transit to the launch zone. Request permission to make ready all missiles in preparation for launch."

"Make ready all missiles," the captain responds.

"Make ready all missiles, aye." Turning to the strike team, I echo the command: "Make ready all missiles."

"Make ready all missiles, aye, ma'am," they respond in a chorus. Even in their exhausted voices, I detect inflections of excitement emerging from their throats. They depart to the corner of Combat where the launch consoles reside, out of the way of other flashing monitors and swirling scopes. One team member tugs at a curtain which surrounds the area, shielding the team's activity from the rest of the crew. Only a select few can enter the sanctuary.

"Strike, a word," the captain says.

"Good luck," Chief whispers, and retreats behind the curtain.

"I need to know you're focused on this launch. No distractions." He looks meaningfully at Blaine, who sits at the TAO console.

"You don't need to worry, sir," I reply. "I'm ready. The team is prepared." My voice sounds too firm to be sincere. The captain raises his wiry eyebrows. He probably thinks I'm disguising nervousness with bravado.

"Yes, but people can freeze when the time comes. Especially…" he stops to clear his throat. "I've seen strike officers who start thinking about the folks on the other end of the shot and get flustered. Drag out the commands. You understand?"

I wait a beat before responding. The captain asks again if I understand.

"They killed my father, sir," I reply. "I thought you'd have heard by now, how people talk on the ship and all."

"No, I didn't know," Captain says.

"He was a firefighter. In the second tower when it collapsed."

The captain stammers, and it thrills me. Despite myself, I smile.

"You don't have to worry about me, sir," I say. "I know who I'm aiming at."

"Lord have mercy," he says, and places his hands on my shoulders. "We're all behind you, Strike."

*

At T-9 hours to launch, the cruise missile checklist requires the strike officer to physically inspect each missile in the launch tubes.

The ship's missile silos remind me of an early-medieval cathedral. Rows of missiles stand upright in their canisters like 20-foot sculptures of saints. Steel uprights guide each warhead in place, intersecting in crosses and arching upward like flying buttresses. Wires wind and bundle around the metal uprights like ornate frescos. I weave through each row, checking missile couplings, making sure each warhead is sound-enough to detonate at its designated time.

FC3 Deacon accompanies me on my checks. Wiry and bespectacled and hook-nosed, she inspects each canister with her piercing gaze, pointing out loose wires and rings of rust I'd otherwise overlook.

"They called the first cruise missiles *revenge weapons*," Deacon says. "They taught us that in strike school. Great name, don't you think, ma'am?"

"Vergeltungswaffen," I reply.

"What?"

"Vergeltungswaffen," I say. "The Germans invented cruise missiles."

"Vergeltungswaffen," she whispers softly to herself, like a secret prayer. Then she asks, "Are you going to write on one of the missiles? Like they did during the first missile strikes of the war?"

The earnestness of her statement jars me. The full force of a nation's vengeance filtered through the hands of a few kids in their early twenties with only Chief and I to guide them.

"No," I say, caressing the missile nearest to me like a holy relic. The next person who touches it, well-what will it be like for them? Quick, I suppose-a flash of light, the sucking of hot air, crushing pressure, the searing pain of blast fragmentation. Not too different from the pain I've carried in my own chest since Dad died.

"What would you write, ma'am?" Deacon asks. "If you could?"

For my father, perhaps. No, that would be inadequate. I'd inscribe a memory instead. From his memorial service. Imprint every emotion onto the missile's metal shell. The feeling of being too stunned and overwhelmed and lost to my own grief to care about anyone else's. I'd add the scents of despair, odors of stale beer, cigarettes, and cheap whiskey on the firefighters' breath as they embraced me through their own charred skin. Men who, in the intervening years, would fall to strange cancers and respiratory ailments, one-by-one.

"Your father was so damn proud of you," they said.

Or: "You go out there and put one right between their eyes for your Da, hear?"

Or: sobbing and incoherent rambling.

I had just finished my first year at the Academy by the time they identified his remains. My mother asked me to wear my dress whites to the service. When I took them off later that night, dusky streaks and handprints anointed my uniform blouse from where these men laid their hands on my back. I feel their weight now, firm and insistent.

"I don't know," I say. "What about you?"

Deacon grins. "I'd draw a huge middle finger."

We continue with our checks.

*

At T-8 hours to launch, the cruise missile checklist recommends you activate the crew rest and provisioning plan. It's going to be a long day. You need the team to be as alert as possible.

I return to my stateroom and let the door swing open behind me. My intent is to shower quickly and grab some coffee before rejoining the team in Combat. Except Blaine walks through the door and lets it click shut behind him.

"Leave that open," I say.

"Relax," he responds. "People will talk no matter what we do."

"People are already talking," I say.

Gossip is a blood sport on deployment. There's not much else to do when trapped on a ship with the same people for months on end. Besides, if you're a woman in the Navy you'll inevitably be the subject of this gossip, be labeled a whore or a bitch. There are too few of us. I attract attention daily from people who don't even realize they're staring. Blaine must know this. It annoys me that he doesn't understand what's at stake. Or that he doesn't care.

"Jokes on them," he says. "It's not like you're sleeping around. With me, at least."

"Doesn't matter," I say.

"Last I checked, I'm the one who's married," he replies. Then, lowering his voice, he says, "Only for a little while longer."

"You're full of shit," I say.

"I'm tired of running, Kira," he says.

Blaine has been running from his divorce for over a year, jumping from deployment to deployment like some wandering Caine on the high seas. He took a set of orders to deploy when his wife announced that she wanted to separate. Divorce proceedings can't occur when either party involved is deployed, he said. But before his ship returned from that deployment, he took orders with another ship, and then another, extending his wife's waiting period. As the third ship commenced its return home, he negotiated orders to meet ours on yet another deployment.

"How long are you going to drag this out?" I asked him one night. We'd snuck out onto the flight deck at night to share a cigarette and talk, our nightly ritual.

"As long as I can," he replied, flicking his spent cigarette into the churning wake below.

"It's spiteful," I said.

"You think I'm that petty?" He asked.

"You're acting like it," I said. That night, I wanted to antagonize him for some reason. To dig underneath his skin and see what lies beneath.

"Look," he replied. "I don't want to get back together with her. That doesn't mean I want things to end, either."

"Why not?" I asked.

"It's a part of my life I'm not ready to see end," he said, then slumped over to light another cigarette, shielding the flame of his lighter from the wind. He remained in this hunched posture without responding. He looked weary. I grabbed his hand to reassure him, nothing more, but something shifted. He looked directly into my eyes, a profound gaze which went beyond his typical liquid-eyed ploys for attention. Then he pulled me to his chest, the cigarette butt still burning in his hand. I breathed in brine from the evening air and the menthol-tinged smoke lingering in the folds of his uniform. We remained in this awkward embrace, neither of us bold enough to do anything else.

We're back in my stateroom. Alone. The door is closed. He gives me this same look now. Wants me to read into his words, to be touched or excited by them, to acknowledge the leap he's just made. My thoughts are too far removed from this moment: I have to launch thirty-three missiles in eight hours.

"I need to focus," I say. "You can't say things like that. Not until after the launch."

"Look, I just wanted to see how you are," he says. His voice is soft and pliable, and I sink into it, let myself be convinced he's looking out for me. I know otherwise. I'm not stupid, just young, so I silence every dissenting voice and surrender.

"I need this," I say. "For revenge or closure or whatever. There's nothing I've wanted more. And now it's here."

"Wanting something and getting it are two separate things," he says. He lays his strong hands on my thighs as he speaks. It's his strength that I find so attractive. And his age. If anything, I wish the ten-year age gap separating us were wider. Older men are always grateful to be in the company of a younger girl, even if she's stocky and covered in rust-colored freckles like I am. Their eagerness excites me.

"I'm not afraid of getting what I want," I say. "I'm afraid of having to chase it for the rest of my life."

"Some people need the chase," he says. "It gives life definition."

I rest my head on his arm. He traces the side of my neck with his lips, grazes my arm with the tips of his fingers, places his head in my lap, wrapping his arms around my waist. His breath passes the fabric of my coveralls, warming the skin on my stomach. This feels different. This feels like reverence. I don't permit myself to act on it. I place my hands on the top of Blaine's head and sit perfectly still.

*

At T-6 hours to launch, I head to the bridge to brief the navigational team about our requirements for launch. I come with our launch parameters and desired wind envelope. The harsh morning sunlight temporarily blinds me when I enter the pilot house.

"Look who decided to grace us with her presence!" The Officer of the Deck says.

"Uh oh, killer on the loose!"

"Girl, you ready for this?"

Despite the mirth in their voices, there's an unmistakable note of jealousy: their jobs are about connecting and repairing, rescuing and maneuvering. Mine is the only job onboard which exists solely for devastation. They make jokes to pretend it doesn't bother them. You can see it in their eyes, though.

That longing and resentment. They look at me like I'm dangerous and defective and delicious all at once. Why wouldn't they? It used to take an entire army to level a city-I can do it with a few clicks of a mouse.

Dad always encouraged my tenacity. He'd goad me on, whether it was to elbow the other players on the field hockey pitch or how to confront the girls at school who kept trying to break into my locker and steal my textbooks.

"You got fight in you, kid," he'd say. "Don't let anyone snuff that out."

Mom disagreed, of course. She counselled restraint and forgiveness and other sanctimonious horseshit. Dad gave me a high-five and poured me a tumbler of Jameson when I came home from a game against North Bergen, pissed we lost, yet proud of having another girl's blood splattered across my jersey. Mom said she wasn't paying private school tuition to perpetuate wild behavior. Dad told me to keep kicking ass and making him proud.

He would've loved to hear about this. Mom didn't understand. After Dad died, she threw herself into volunteering with a local refugee resettlement charity. She remarried last year to some guy named R.J. whom she met at her church bereavement group. A plumber who lost his wife to cancer. Mom asked me to be happy for her, to understand her need for peace. Said she and R.J. prayed nightly for my reconciliation with the past. I asked her what kind of adult man walks around asking people to call him R.J.

"Alright, guys, in six hours we'll be launching an attack using all the cruise missiles in our inventory," I say. "The good news is you get the best view in the house. The bad news is you're going to have to do exactly what I say from down in Combat. One misstep and we'll end up putting a bird through a school instead of our intended target. I need all of you to keep an eye on the surface picture. Let us know if there are any small boats getting in the way. Keep our speed to less than five knots."

"Yes, ma'am!" someone cries out and renders a mock salute.

"Light their asses up, Strike!" says another.

"Oh, one more thing," I say before I depart the bridge. "Captain will be up to confirm, but we're authorized to take down any small boats that try to get in our way. That means you can make-ready the 50 cal."

Their celebratory shouts follow me as I exit the bridge.

*

At T-4 hours to launch, the strike team reassembles in Combat to activate the strike package. The next time we depart the curtained area, we will have destroyed an entire terrorist compound.

"Those dick nuggets down in the galley are refusing to send us dinner before the strike," Chief Bishop says as I join the team. "How are we supposed blow shit up when half the team is starving?"

Growing up, my mother told me that pious women never swore. Somehow, I think even God would tremble in the face of one of Chief Bishop's rants.

"Relax, Chief," I tell her. "I asked the wardroom guys to send down meals for the team."

"I don't say this often enough, Strike," Chief says. "But you have a brain in your head. Surprising for an officer."

"I brought you some coffee, too."

"Thanks be to Jesus. You are a saint, ma'am." She accepts the cup I offer her with two hands and makes a bowing motion.

"The patron saint of cruise missiles," I respond. "I like the sound of that."

"Let's see how the next few hours go," Chief replies. After a few sips of the coffee, she asks, "You ready?"

"Yes," I say. "I'm tired of everyone asking me this."

"Little less attitude, ma'am. I don't mean for the launch. I've seen that mean streak in you. Everyone in this bullshit profession forgets us females got more anger to let out than most."

"Then what do you mean?" I ask.

"The aftermath. They're probably gonna give you some officer of the year award and put your ginger ass on the front page of every recruiting poster."

"I'm sure the Navy has better cover models," I say. "You've done more strikes than I have. Why not you?"

"Because I'm not a college-educated white girl," she says. I look down and shake my head. Chief laughs at me.

"Loosen up a bit, Strike. We're not doing anything serious. Just dropping a few hundred pounds of explosives on some bad guys."

"Did I ever tell you about my dad?" I ask.

"I heard about it," she says. "Nothing's a secret around here."

She taps the checklist lying on the plotting table in front of us. It has Blaine's name written on top as the TAO assigned to assist with the strike. She raises her eyebrows at me as she does so. I pretend not to notice.

"How about you?" I ask. "You ever feel any remorse?"

"Sometimes," Chief says. "It can tear you up inside. Back during the initial invasion, when things were really hot, I was doing one of these a day for eight months straight but didn't get to thinking about it until we got home. Then I got pretty low. Took me a good three or four months to get my mind right. I mean, causing all this havoc? Just wasn't the way I was brought up."

"Me either," I say. "But I've wanted this moment. For years now. It sounds savage, but if I didn't get this chance, it'd probably consume me. That make me a bad person?"

Chief shrugs. "Who knows what's good and bad anymore. I get less and less sure of that as I get older. I mean, the people we're targeting. They look more like me than you do. Makes me wonder whose side I'm on."

"What gets you through it?" I ask.

"My grandmother never voted," she says. "She grew up in Mississippi. Was too scared to do so, even after she moved to Chicago in the '80s. Spent half her life unable to get to the polls, the other half afraid of what would happen if she did."

I shake my head but say nothing.

"Earlier this morning, I started praying for the people we're about to hit, their souls and all," Chief continues. "Then I remembered Nan. How she lived her life terrified. There's gratification in giving it to these bastards. Stop a different bunch of folks from pulling the same shit somewhere else."

"That's something," I say.

"Maybe," she replies. "Or maybe the world is fucked up because we run around settling our scores with the wrong people."

"What's the alternative?" I ask. "Forgive and forget? Turn the other cheek?"

"Ma'am, I have whiplash from turning the other cheek so often," Chief says.

We both laugh and return to the checklist. It is time to begin. We move into a trance. A meditative state of concentration. A fundamentalist's adherence to the launch doctrine. I issue a command and Chief repeats it, she passes the order along to the rest of the team, and they respond in kind. We chant engagement numbers and coordinates; it becomes an invocation designed to conjure fiery retribution.

"Activate strike package," I say.

"Activate the strike package, aye! Activating the strike package!" Four voices echo in reply.

"Very well," I say.

*

"Attention Strike Team, we are at T-60 minutes to launch," I call out.

"T-60 minutes, aye," the team responds.

I shift my weight from leg to leg and roll my ankles. Three hours without sitting takes its toll. My hips ache and my lower back screams at me for relief. My head throbs. I close my eyes imagine the moment of launch: the steady reverberation and unmistakable sound of boosters igniting, the caustic smell of burning propellant. This meditation chases away all discomfort.

"I'll call the old man," I say to Chief. She nods. The captain picks up his phone halfway through the second ring.

"It's time, sir," I say. "We need you in Combat for final validation."

"On my way," he says. "Strike?"

"Sir?"

"This is big."

"I know, sir."

"No, I...I want to say, you've done well."

He waits for me to thank him or tell him I appreciate his support. My mind is on the checklist. On the missiles spinning in their canisters. On the sucking pain in my chest. On the men three hundred miles away whose bodies I'll tear apart with pressurized gas and metal. On the peace it will bring me.

"We'll be standing by for your arrival, sir," I reply, and hang up the phone.

*

At T-30 minutes, the ceremony is proceeding smoothly. There have been no connectivity issues. All the missions upload without incident. The bridge reports a clear surface picture. Team members check and re-check their co-ordinates. The captain sits in the corner, reviewing our launch documents. Chief and I peek over team members' shoulders and compulsively review the checklist. There is tension, but it is an orderly tension. Vengeance feels like an inevitability.

Blaine wanders over from the TAO console.

"This is it," he says softly. He places his hand on my shoulder. The firmness of his grasp is a contrast to the tremors shooting up and down my spine. "You're shaking," he says.

"Am I?" I lean back into him. His body seems to absorb my tremors. We stand there, together, shaking.

*

At T-10 minutes to launch, the engagements emerge quickly. You can't issue a single order to send 33 missiles flying at the same time. Chief and I approve each engagement separately, a frenzy of clicking mouses and shuffling papers. Orders flow from our mouths like mystic intonation.

"Attention Strike Team, we are at T-10 minutes to launch," I say.

"T-10-minute, aye, ma'am," is the response. Intensity saturates their voices.

"Initiate final checks," I call out again.

"Initiate final checks, aye," they echo back.

Somewhere, from behind the curtain, I hear cheers and claps, followed by Blaine's voice yelling for silence.

"Final checks complete," Deacon calls out.

"Very well," I reply.

Each minute feels like a minor agony. We have nothing to do now but wait until the appointed time. I call up to the bridge and tell them to verify whether the booster drop zone is clear. Aside from this, no one says a word. We fall into an anticipatory silence, listening only to the hum of the ventilation.

The appointed moment arrives.

"Ma'am," Deacon calls loudly, even though Chief and I are standing directly behind her. "Request permission to execute engagement seven-three-two."

"Execute engagement seven-three-two," I say. Chief lays one hand on my arm the other on Deacon's shoulder. I grasp her arm and place my hand on Deacon's other shoulder. There we stand, consubstantial in destruction. Deacon moves her cursor across the screen and clicks it three times.

"Weapon is away," Deacon says.

Each engagement arrives in furious succession thereafter. The order to execute emanates not from my mouth, but from someplace deep within my chest.

"Request permission to execute engagement four-one-zero."

"Request permission to execute engagement nine-zero-eight."

I move from console to console as if in a trance, delivering words which will seal someone's fate. Which will free me from mine.

"Engagement nine-zero-four, ready for review."

"Stand by for quick tasking, engagement three-two-one."

The ship shutters as the first missile ignites and soars from the launcher. We feel the roar as much as we hear it, even though we are deep within the skin of the ship. A violent rumble rattles the air around us.

"Engagement two-oh-one."

"Engagement six-oh-nine."

The bridge team notifies us as each booster drops into the water below. The residual ripples rock the ship back and forth. More cheers erupt from behind the curtain. Blaine quiets them. The ship continues to convulse.

With each salvo released, I wait for the ensuing ecstasy, the dissolution of the clawing rage and oppressive grief I carried inside me for so long. Except these feelings only intensify. There is no peace, only the sound of my father's voice telling me to get up or I'll be late for school. The taste of his omelets, thick with too much cheese yet soggy with too many tomatoes. The scratch of the ever-present callus on his right thumb whenever he held my hand. The recognizable echo of his voice across a soccer field. These memories serve only to suffocate. There is heat and pressure crushing my chest, an inward tearing with no release. The weight of the hands on my back press harder and harder until I feel as if I might explode.

The ship falls silent. The thunder reverberating around us dulls to a soft rumble, then a murmur, then fades entirely.

"Strike package complete," Deacon says. "We did it, ma'am. We did it."

The crew breaks into applause. Whistles and shouts rise from the passageways outside Combat. Each member of the Strike team stands, high fiving each other, disrupting the ritual with raucousness.

"Well done, Strike," the captain says. "You should be proud."

Blaine bursts through the curtain and wraps me in a hug, not caring about the stares he attracts from the captain and the rest of the team. He notices my stiffness and pulls away.

"It didn't work, Blaine" I say.

"Kira, the strike was a success," he says. "We'll get damage assessments shortly."

"It's still there," I reply, suddenly aware of how painful it feels to draw breath.

*

The cruise missile checklist recommends the Strike team be exempt from evening watches after a launch so they can catch up on sleep and be on alert for follow-on tasking. You never know when more launch assignments will arrive.

Instead of returning to my stateroom, I slip into Blaine's-his roommate is covering his watch-and close the door behind me. He smiles and opens his arms. I walk into them. Wordlessly, we heap our clothes on a nearby chair. Search each other's bodies without admiration. The act feels desperate, the frantic coupling of two people unaccustomed to one another, yet, with eyes shut, incapable of learning. We lay there afterward, tightly pressed together less out of affection than the lack of space afforded by the narrow rack. Neither of us finish. We simply stop at some point, unwilling to go on.

As I lay there, I close my eyes and recall the missiles' deafening ignition, the all-encompassing thunder, desperately searching for some meaning in it. All I hear is empty clamor.

TROU

Leave it to the Service Academies to fuck up misogyny. Sexist slurs are a proud export of each institution, yet no one discusses how awkward they all are. For example, Air Force Academy cadets refer to the women in their ranks as "cockpits." Too on the nose, if you ask me, though I suppose most slanderous terms don't deal in nuance. The Naval Academy, my alma mater, refers to women as "Wubas," an acronym for "women used by all" or "women with unusually big asses," depending on the speaker's preferred method of disdain. The best insults rarely require three sentences to explain, though.

West Point cadets call women "trou," short for "trousers." The implication being that women are like trousers: everyone gets in a pair. As a metaphor, it just doesn't work. Pair is a double entendre for breasts or balls; even the most sexually ignorant cadet must know that's not where you "get in." And why trousers? It's too old-fashioned, even for a chauvinistic epithet. I don't think I could be upset if someone called me a "stupid trou" or whatever adjective that would inevitably precede it. The other expressions have their bite, however minor. But trou? I'd probably laugh.

Midshipman Conner didn't laugh. She smashed a ceramic plate over Midshipman Villers' head, requiring him to be sent to Brigade Medical for twenty stitches. The corpsmen shaved the top of Villers' head, but not the sides, making him look like a pissed-off Capuchin monk. And so this squabble became my problem to manage as their company officer.

Naval Academy protocol states that all incidents of assault need to be immediately reported to our battalion officer, which brought me to Commander Lionel "Lion" Bernhart's office at three-thirty on a Friday afternoon. Lion had already abandoned his uniform and slipped into a collared shirt and khaki shorts. He invited me to sit, though he stared longingly at the golf clubs tucked in the corner of his office the entire time I spoke.

"This sounds like a clear case of assault, Lieutenant DiMare," Lion said, slapping the sides of his chair to signal his imminent departure. "One midshipman attacked another. Villers…he's on the football team, no? Their officer representative will weigh in on this one. Good man, that Colonel Bingsley. Let's send the separation paperwork up to the commandant for review."

Staff at the Academy use the official military term "separation" instead of expulsion, as if we were merely removing a bad orange from the rest of the bushel. In the pocket of my khaki uniform pants, my phone vibrated. I silenced it, only to have it buzz again.

"It's not that simple, sir," I replied. "Midshipman Conner is claiming she struck Villers because he was sexually harassing her. Besides. Villers is only a place kicker."

"Oh," he said. "That's different." He looked at his clubs again and heaved a sigh which fluttered the papers on his desk.

"Assault is rarely convenient, Lion," I said.

Lion scowled. I couldn't help myself. He had a pair of Oakleys perched on top of his head, for Christ's sake. My phone buzzed anew. Lion asked if I needed to answer it. I said no.

"Do you think her claim is valid?" he asked. "Or is she just trying to deflect blame?"

"I'm looking into it, sir," I said. "I have all the paperwork here for their disciplinary hearing. If your schedule allows, we can run it on Monday."

"I'll tell you what, DiMare," Lion replied, heaving a sigh of relief. "Sounds like you've got it under control. So how about this—let's have you adjudicate the case on your own."

"Conduct the hearing myself?"

"Yes."

"Sir, cases involving assault are supposed to be dealt with at the battalion level. Like you said, the commandant will have to sign off on it."

"Well," Lion stood as he replied, signaling that it was time for me to leave. "It'll be my signature on the final verdict, of course. I trust you'll make the right decision. Think of it as a development opportunity. You'll know what to do."

I had no idea what to do. But there I sat, regardless, with Conner and Villers in my office staring at me expectantly, as if I magically controlled their futures. And I could, really. The thought made my hand itch for one of the mini bottles of Smirnoff I stashed in my bottom desk drawer. God, I couldn't wait until they left my office so I could take a sip.

"I informed my coaching staff about this situation," Midshipman Villers said. He thrust out his thinly muscled chest and twisted his mouth downward into a perfect u-shape. I could completely understand why Conner slugged him. "Including our O-rep, Colonel Bingsley."

Damn. It took Villers five minutes in my office before he mentioned he was a member of the football team. My friend Taylor bet me $20 that Villers would mention he played football within the first ten minutes of our meeting; I said he'd at least wait twenty. At the far end of my desk, my cellphone vibrated. I turned it face down.

"I hope you mentioned the part where you deserved it," Midshipman Conner replied. She avoided making eye contact with either me or Villers.

"I don't take kindly to false accusations."

"Then quit making them!"

"Or what, you'll attack me again? Come and try it."

"Both of you, knock it off!" I yelled. They started and stared back at me with wide eyes. My phone buzzed two times in quick succession. "Villers, I'm sure you have a supportive coaching staff, but we handle conduct issues within the chain of command, okay? And Conner, who else was at the table? I'm going to need additional witness statements."

"Why are you the one collecting statements?" Villers asked, making no attempt to disguise the accusatory tone in his voice.

"Excuse me?"

Villers shrugged. "I just think it's a little unfair for you to be the one to sort this out with you being a fee-male and all." He spat the word with such derision, I almost leaped from my seat.

"Know what? You need some time to cool off. You're on restriction this weekend for insubordination."

"Are you kidding me? Ma'am, I had to get stitches. I have a sprained neck..."

"Stop talking," I bellowed. Villers jumped. *That's right, you little shit,* I thought. *Didn't think someone my size could yell this loudly, did you?*

He regained his composure and clenched his fists and jaw. Conner smirked as she looked at the ground. Her muddy blonde hair frizzed at the crown despite being pulled into a tight bun at the back of her head, encircling her face in a crazed halo.

"You're not off the hook, Conner," I said. "I want you both back in here on Monday. We'll adjudicate then. In the meantime, stay the hell away from each other. Is that clear?"

They each mumbled a downtrodden, "Yes, ma'am." I dismissed them, shut the door behind them, dug two mini-bottles of vodka—one for each of my unruly charges—from under the files in my drawer and downed them in quick succession. I typically try not to drink at work, I really do. Then something like this happens and I'm left with no other choice. And then there's my goddamn phone.

Despite myself, I read the texts.

Farfalle it's not a good day I need to speak with you.

YOUR FATHER IS GETTING MARRIED THIS WEEKEND.

Your sister is going. Did she tell you?

I need to hear your voice.

WHERE ARE YOU????

Farfalle, can you pick up please…

A text from Taylor rounded out the barrage of messages. *What's the latest on the Midshipmen fight club?*

I downed a third bottle and got to work.

Each witness I called into my office proved to be worthless. None of the other midshipmen who sat at the lunch table with Villers and Conner seemed to hear any of their conversation. One witness said Villers was "just joking around" but didn't elaborate. Another said Villers had been talking about women who participated in combat positions, but then the kid seemingly contracted amnesia and couldn't remember anything else. Of the ten midshipmen who sat at the table, none claimed to notice anything unusual until Conner, who sat next to Villers, flung the pasty lasagna off her plate, stood, and brought the ceramic plate down upon his head.

In her written statement, Conner claimed Villers routinely made offensive remarks at meals since the start of the semester two months ago. He'd tell stories about visiting other colleges on the weekend, for example, and say how good it was *to get to see women who weren't ugly or fat*, while casting a meaningful glance in her direction. According to Conner, Villers would prattle about how so-and-so girl from another company was a slut, or how unbelievably stupid this girl in his political science class was. She tried to brush it off, she said, but he just kept running his mouth. The breaking point came, as Conner indicated in her statement, when Villers brought up his brother who was graduating from West Point last year:

> *He started saying that his brother wanted some kind of role but didn't end up with a spot because they gave them away to women who didn't deserve it. He said women had completely different physical requirements and how unfair it all was. I try not to talk about topics like that, because I know the others don't agree with me, but that was all too much. I don't think they took anyone's spot, Villers's brother is probably just mad about losing his, if he's anything like his brother. No one else said anything, so I spoke up. I said his brother hadn't done anything meaningful in his career and had no place to criticize these women. Villers then told me to shut up because I had no idea what I was talking*

about and in the words of his brother I was just some "hideous trou." The entire squad laughed. I'm not proud of it, but I lost control in the moment and hit him.

After reading her statement, I reviewed Conner's record. Her grades looked fine—far fewer A's than C's—but passing. She played rugby, volunteered at a local elementary school, helped the plebes during their weekend training. Seemed to be generally liked without being overwhelmingly popular. Villers' record looked similarly bland. A political science major with decent grades for a football player. Did a year at the preparatory school before arriving at the Academy and started as a place kicker since his Youngster year. Had a brother who graduated from West Point and a father who graduated from Navy twenty-five years ago. Villers spent most of his time with the football team and had only been sitting with his squad because the team didn't eat lunch together during the off season.

Damn. I hoped to find something to indicate a pattern for either of them. No such luck.

How this glorified babysitting gig is seen as prestigious, I'll never know. Sure, the campus is beautiful, if a little pretentious with its neoclassical white marble structures. In terms of authority, I'm free to run my company in the manner of my choosing as long as the midshipmen who report to me stay out of trouble and get good grades, which typically isn't hard. They're all post-adolescent overachievers and incorrigible brown-nosers. Much different from back when I was a midshipman. I spent most of my time figuring out where I could drink underage without getting caught.

I owe you ten dollars, I texted Taylor. *Drinks at Davis later?*

I ignored my mother's texts.

I'm down, he texted back along with a ribbon of beer mug emojis.

I spun in my chair to look out of the window behind my desk. The view was one of the few perks of working here. Beyond the sprawling athletic fields abutting the building where I worked, the Severn River stretched out, unimpeded, until it flowed into the brackish Chesapeake Bay. Though cold, the day was clear, and as the mid-afternoon sun reflected off the river, flecks of piercing silver light radiated into the office.

God, how I wanted to be out on the water now. Life at sea is rigorous, but it isn't complex. There's a peacefulness to it. Your routine separates you from your thoughts. I would've stayed on sea duty for another four years if the Navy let me—I even volunteered to do so. But then my old commanding officer, Commander Depford, called me into his cabin to discuss my options for a shore assignment.

"You're on the fast track, Sofia," Commander Depford said, pointing meaningfully to the performance review he held in his hand. "You'll make a stellar department head and a great commanding officer one day. But we need to talk about that night in Oman."

"I'm not sure what more needs to be said, sir," I replied. "It was a night of poor judgment. I've learned a lot from it."

This was all a lie, of course. I learned nothing from that evening, except that I can handle my alcohol better than most grown men.

"Sofia," Depford said. He pronounced my name like a disappointed parent, which made me want to flip my chair over and stomp out of the room. Every other Commanding Officer I worked with applied a compassionate detachment in their dealings with the wardroom. They needed you to do a job, so you did it. Depford, on the other hand, had a grating habit of treating everyone like an actual person.

"Sofia," he continued. "You were returned to the ship by shore patrol for making politically insensitive remarks about the Sultan."

God help me, I laughed.

"You could have gotten arrested," Commander Depford continued.

"Not really a sign of a secure ruler," I said. "If the Sultan can't take a joke."

"Well, the ravings of an intoxicated American woman won't change that."

"I read he's actually quite lovely," I said apologetically. "Progressive in his own way."

"Let's leave the Sultan out of it. The incident was completely out of character for you," Depford replied. "Is everything alright?"

"Just let myself get carried away, sir," I said. "As did the rest of the wardroom. But I was also the only one who got up on time the next day and did my job."

Depford shook his head, probably because he knew I was right. The entire wardroom got sloshed that evening. We pulled into a resort town in Oman after four months straight at sea and let ourselves get a little too loose at a bar in some fancy resort. Our weapons officer sucker punched an Australian drinking nearby, who promptly laid him flat in return. Our admin officer drank so much that he shat himself, shrugged when we pointed it out, and threw back another round while mired in his own filth. Our communications officer and auxiliaries officer ended up making out with each other in the middle of the hotel lobby, ignoring the hotel concierge's angry shouts for them to stop. While waiting for the liberty van back to the ship, our training officer vomited in a wicker wastepaper basket, unaware of the mess oozing all over the floor. Every one of them failed to show up to muster the next morning. Except me. I stood alone with the commanding officer on the flight deck, feeling like roadkill and wondering where everyone was.

Yet I was the one who got in trouble when all I did was say (albeit somewhat loudly, while standing on a bar stool) that the Sultan is a real son of a bitch if he doesn't let his own people criticize him in the press. Then I started singing whatever fragmented verses of *La Marseillaise* I could remember. I'm glad shore patrol picked me up shortly thereafter. My French is terrible.

"You manage yourself well. You know your stuff and people listen to you because of it. But you have to learn different ways to lead. How to bring people along. Guide them. Being the smartest and the toughest isn't always enough," Depford said. "Your shore tour is coming up. Have you thought about being a company officer?"

"I'd rather throw myself into the ship's propeller," I said.

Depford laughed. "Well, I'd like you to reconsider," he said.

Ten days later, I received my assignment: Company Officer, United States Naval Academy. No way this happened by accident. There's supposed to be an application process to land this gig. Depford probably called in a favor with my detailer to have my orders changed. Nice guys are always the biggest assholes.

*

My office phone rang. An internal number. *Athletic Department* flashed across the caller ID.

"Hello, is this Lieutenant DiMare?" A gruff voice shouted from the other end of the phone. He pronounced my name "dee mare," as if pointing at a female horse. "This is Colonel Bingsley calling about Midshipman Villers."

"Um, hi, Colonel. Guess you're calling about the incident?"

"Yes, Lieutenant. I was expecting a call earlier."

"Notifying the athletic department isn't typically a part of our protocol."

"I see," Bingsley crooned. "Well, we're talking now. How is this being handled?"

"I'm looking into this very closely, sir," I said, making a face behind the phone. Immature, I know, but the vodka had made my face start to glow, and his condescending voice rankled me. "Reviewing statements from witnesses and will present the findings to my battalion officer on Monday."

"I'd expect something this serious to be wrapped up over the weekend," Bingsley said. "Lion's an old friend of mine. My next call will be to him."

"I already discussed this with Lion," I replied. "He agreed this is serious enough to warrant a thorough look." The "thorough" fell bluntly from my mouth. My tongue felt heavy and sticky, like I was carving out words with a butter knife. My pulse quickened.

"Let me be clear—we start spring training next week. I'd like to have this wrapped up beforehand."

"We tend not to allow football schedules to dictate procedures, sir," I said. "Both parties need some time to cool off over the weekend. And like I said, I need time to look at all the facts."

"Villers was assaulted."

"It isn't that straightforward. You see..."

"A young man is assaulted and that's not straightforward enough? Unacceptable. I'll escalate this to the commandant. You can't tell me..."

He continued his tirade, shouting "unacceptable!" over and over. I put the receiver down for about a minute to let him vent, cracked open a fourth mini bottle from my desk, and drained the contents as he finished.

"Sir, Villers was struck after he sexually harassed one of his classmates," I replied.

"Oh," Bingsley replied after a pause. "I hadn't heard that."

"No, sir, I suspect you didn't," I said, smiling.

"That...doesn't sound like him. Don't get me wrong, I'm not unsympathetic. I have two daughters at home."

"That's nice."

"Still, you can see how one of our team members getting physically assaulted would concern me."

"I'd imagine it would," I said. "No need for concussions off the field, too."

Bingsley snorted, but otherwise remained quiet. I gripped the phone until my knuckles turned white.

How many times have I been here, I thought. Dictated to and undermined by men who thought they knew better. Even Bingsley, a man I couldn't see and probably would never meet, felt the need to tell me how I needed to do my job, one I never wanted in the first place but ended up in because another man thought it would be good for me.

"Colonel," I said through gritted teeth, finally breaking the tense silence. "You're looking out for Villers. I appreciate that. But I have to look out for him and the other midshipman involved. Like I said, I'm investigating. There will be consequences, we just need to figure out what's appropriate given the circumstances."

"I'll be calling on Monday to verify that's the case. And I expect you to email me the case information by the end of the day," he said, then abruptly hung up, leaving me alone with an absent hum on the other end of the phone.

I looked at the clock: quarter past five. *Bingsley could wait until Monday for the files*, I thought, and tossed my empty bottles into the purple canvas bag I took with me to work each day. Couldn't risk throwing them away here.

*

Taylor awaited me in the back of the bar when I arrived, two tumblers of whiskey ready. The bar was loud and dark and unassuming, which kept away D.C. day-trippers and deterred presumptuous Annapolitans with their stupid boat shoes and blank-eyed golden retrievers. We could soak up decent whiskey with reliably good hamburgers and blend undetected into the background, unobserved by midshipmen or their visiting parents.

I sat on the same side of the booth as Taylor so I could weigh in on the photos he swiped on his phone.

"He seems too high maintenance," I commented on the image Taylor showed me.

"Yeah, but that's just because he has money," Taylor said. "Look at what he's wearing. That's actual money, not one of those guys who dresses flashy to pretend. His loafers are Ferragamo. Slightly worn, too."

"So?"

"They'd be pristine Gucci if he was pretending," Taylor said. "Wealth whispers, my dear. Didn't your mother ever teach you that?"

"My mother shopped at Sears, not Neiman's," I said. Which wasn't entirely true. Before my father left, she preferred Bloomingdale's. She supervised every class trip I had in elementary school with a fresh blowout, wearing heels and low-cut tops and her enormous yellow gold Bulgari earrings, the ones that made every other mom in school seethe with jealousy. I noticed it even as a kid, how they sneered and stared a little too long whenever she turned her back on them. Then my father ran off with one of the dental hygienists who worked in his office shortly after my fourteenth birthday. She had to sell those earrings to cover the mortgage payments. To spite her for some reason I've since forgotten, my father had started sending his alimony checks to Middletown, Ohio instead of Middletown, New Jersey. She cried for a solid hour in the parking lot of the jewelry store after she sold them, hyperventilating and unable to steady her hand long enough to put the car key in the ignition. I drove her home, even though I didn't have my permit yet.

"That explains so much," Taylor said, casting a critical eye to my jeans and fleece jacket. "I worry about you, you know. We spend hours going over my prospects. But yours? I can't be the only man in your life."

"Other men are too difficult," I said, nudging him with my shoulder. Taylor and I knew each other back on my old ship. We were friendly, though he typically kept his distance from the rest of the wardroom. When we both received orders back to the Naval Academy for our shore assignments—him as an instructor in the systems engineering department, me as a company officer—we made the decision to live with each other more out of practicality than genuine affection. Now we sat side-by-side in the same booth, our arms woven together, faces flushed with the pleasant feeling of tipsiness creeping into intoxication, jointly deciding on which man Taylor should hook up with this weekend.

"I'm serious, Sof," he said. "You're going to grow cobwebs down there."

"Sex only brings problems," I replied. "Case in point—you're screwed if anyone sees you on there."

"That's the point," Taylor said.

"I'm being serious, Tay," I replied.

"Whoever finds me would be guilty of searching on it themselves," he said. "That's the beauty of this app."

"Would you put it beyond someone to try and trap you? This profession's riddled with assholes, Taylor," I said.

"Really, Sof? Tell me more about being gay in the Navy," he replied. Even though he spoke playfully, he whispered the implicating word. I could tell I was getting on his nerves.

"You know what I mean," I said. "I'd hate to have to find another room-mate."

"Awww, it's like you care," Taylor said, smiling. "Has the Madwoman in the Wardroom finally grown a heart?"

"Don't be a dick," I said.

"Hey, that's what they called you, you know," he said. "Back on the ship. The Madwoman in the Wardroom. Think it started after that night in Oman."

"Well aware," I said. "I've been unlucky with nicknames."

"Oh, that's right. Doesn't your mother call you spaghetti or something?"

"Farfalle, you Wasp," I replied. "Like the bow-tie pasta."

"Why?"

"Because I'm shaped like it," I said.

Look at you! I remember her exclaiming. *Hippy and busty and skinny in the middle. I'd have killed for a figure like that at your age.* Then her eyes would glaze over, and she'd get teary and say, *Your father always preferred slender women. Men with money always want their women little. You'll need to make your own, Farfalle. For both of us.*

"That's amazing," Taylor said. "I need to meet Mama DiMare one day."

"You're not missing much," I replied, downing the rest of my drink, and waving to the bartender for another.

We walked the mile back to our townhouse, arm in arm to keep our-selves upright for the duration of the walk. Laughing like maniacs as we hobbled along, each of Taylor's long, languid strides accounting for at least three of my rapid ones.

"What happened with that girl in your company, by the way?" Taylor asked. "All the mids in my class were talking about it today. Said she went psycho on that football player."

"He's a just placekicker. And he deserved it. Lion's making me adjudicate it myself."

"Well, aren't you important now," he said.

"It's mildly terrifying, Taylor. I got a call from their O-rep today, who is a Colonel, of course, and not afraid to throw his weight around. The whole thing feels like a trap," I said, choking on my last sentence. My emotions suddenly felt sharper and more pronounced, the very thing I'd been trying to drink away. Knew I should've gone for another round at the bar.

"Probably is," he said. "But to hell with them. It's your decision."

"Yeah, but they're testing me to see if I'll make the right one," I said. Taylor wouldn't get it. He was the only child of two adoring parents who bought him a car after graduation and still helped him with his credit card payments even though he turned twenty-seven last month. Meanwhile, I kept my spending to a minimum so I could keep my mom's electricity running. Taylor slapped backs and smoked cigars with the rest of the military staff without raising suspicions about his weekend activities; those same people surveyed me critically whenever I entered a room.

"Hey," Taylor said, suddenly serious. "You're going to be fine. Sure, you dress like shit and you live like a drunken nun. But you can do anything, Sof. I mean, you almost started a coup in Oman."

"That was just me running my mouth," I said.

"No, Oman was something different. You were on a rampage. What set you off?"

I said I didn't remember and asked if he was going to message the guy in the Ferragamo shoes. He winked at me and told me he already did.

Taylor shuffled off to bed as soon as we got back to the house. He said he wanted to work out in the morning and burn off the alcohol if the guy on the app did end up replying. It was early still, only about ten-thirty, so I hopped into bed as well, and grabbed the bottle of vodka I stashed behind my nightstand and did what I'd put off doing all day. I called my mother.

She picked up the phone mid-sentence, as if she started her wailing as soon as she saw my name on the screen.

"Couldn't even marry the woman he ruined my life over," she said. I could barely understand her ravings through my own drunken fog, but I pieced it together, word-by-slurred-word. "*Our* lives, Farfalle. Our lives. She's in her thirties, you know. Closer to your age than mine. Disguising son-of-a-bitch."

"Jeanie called to ask for my address for the invitation," I said.

"Doing Daddy's bidding," my mother said. I drank steadily during her rant, savoring the searing sensation the vodka ignited in my chest and stomach.

"Spoiled little brat," she continued. "Sucking up to Daddy so he pays for her condo."

"And her baby shower," I said.

"I'm glad there's still you, Farfalle," my mom responded. "Always my good girl."

I took another long sip.

Before Jeanie called to tell me about our father's wedding, I hadn't spoken with my older sister in over a year. It suited her well to be on Daddy's side and I let her know I thought she was a spineless shit because of it. Still, you couldn't blame her for being pragmatic. Choosing my mom after the divorce meant I had to find my own way to pay for college and give up half my paycheck once I graduated to keep Mom solvent. I'm sure dignity is worth something. It sure as shit isn't paying my rent, though.

*

The next morning, I woke up to Taylor digging through my closet. I must've fallen asleep while I was on the phone with my mom because I found it in the middle of the bed, wrapped around the flat sheet, battery entirely drained. I found the emptied bottle under there too, but left it in place and fought my way out of the tangle of covers I'd wound around myself during the night. The room seemed too bright, even though I'd shut the curtains and had my comforter pulled over my head. The possibility of seeing daylight made my eyes throb and pulse at the sockets. My limbs felt stiff and rigid and ready to crumble.

"What are you doing?" I asked Taylor when I'd finally freed my head. I still hadn't opened my eyes.

"Oh good, you are alive," he said. "I was ready to put a mirror under your nose."

"What time is it?"

"You don't want to know. Anyway, I'm borrowing a bag. Dylan texted me back and we're getting together later tonight."

"Dylan?"

"Ferragamo loafers. My overnight bags are all too nice. I need something in the back of the car that looks casual, but not like I was expecting to stay the night."

"Right." A haggard groan escaped my mouth as I sat up.

"You look terrible," he said. "Since when do you get this hung over after a few drinks?"

"I'm just tired," I said. "Long week. There's a backpack on the top shelf."

"Found it. It's torn on one side. Seriously, Sof. You're not in college anymore. Start investing in adult clothes," Taylor said. He threw up his hands, then turned to face me. "I'll get you some water."

"I love you," I said, throwing the covers back over my head. I heard his footsteps plod away on the worn carpet, then stop.

"Wait," Taylor said. "This purple bag in the corner. Are you using this?"

"Don't…" I called out, springing out of bed despite my cracking bones. But I rose a second too late. He had already dumped out the contents onto the floor, then looked back at me with his enormous eyes as a dozen mini bottles of Smirnoff fell out as well. I hadn't realized I finished that many until I saw them bounce and roll on faded gray carpet.

"Isn't this your work bag?" he asked. I recognized some solemn and stern tone in his voice, a strange sound to hear emerging from Taylor's mouth.

"Yeah," I said. "Those were from a while ago, though." I laughed briefly afterward, a short, timid chuckle. Taylor only frowned.

"Sof, this is…a lot," he replied.

"It isn't like I finished them all in one sitting," I replied.

"You do this during the day? You know if one of the mids catches you, it'd be all of five minutes before they tell everyone."

"Look who's lecturing who about caution," I said. "Honestly, they were in there for so long I forgot all about them."

"Thing is," he said. "I don't believe you."

"I don't give a shit if you do," I replied. "You have the easy shore assignment." "Whoa, okay, let's slow down for a second," Taylor said.

"I'm not going to be lectured to. Not by you. You know nothing about what it takes to stay sane in this bullshit job."

"Know what, Sof, if that's the way you see it, it's your life," he said. "But I'm not going to pretend I approve, either." He put his hands up and walked backwards out of my room.

"Oh, spare me your righteous disapproval," I called after him. My voice sounded both hoarse and high-pitched somehow. No. I wasn't going to listen to this.

Taylor didn't respond, which only enraged me more, so I yelled even louder, following him into his room as he started to pack. He abandoned my bag and picked up one of his own instead, a large leather weekender. "What are your little weekend escapades if not your own outlet?"

"Don't you dare," he said sharply. "That's different and you know it."

"Really? Do your dating in the open, do you?"

"That's low," he said. "And this isn't about me. Believe it or not, I want to help. Look around. Who else is there, Sof?"

"You're being a righteous prick about it," I replied.

"Alright, Sofia," Taylor said calmly. "I'm not talking to you when you're like this. How about we try later, okay?"

He didn't look at me as he folded clothes and neatly tucked them inside his bag. I continued yelling at him, saying he had no idea what he was talking about, that he was making assumptions he couldn't back up, and Jesus, why was he being so judgmental? He didn't respond, except to murmur, "Okay, Sof," intermittently. Finally, he zipped the bag, slung it over his shoulders, and headed downstairs toward the door. Before he left, I grabbed a shoe I'd left in the entryway and flung it at him, hitting him just below the nape of his neck.

Taylor paused for a moment, then turned around slowly, shoulders tensed to his ears. He looked as if he would say something. That I was crazy, that he was moving out. Anything, really. I wanted him to respond. He didn't. He simply shook his head and walked out of the door.

As soon as the door closed, I wanted to scream. To run into the kitchen and pull each drawer open and slam it shut over and over until the clamor of the silverware melted into my own inarticulate screams. My anger never exploded. It always folded inward. So I grabbed my car keys and headed to the nearest liquor store for a few bottles of cheap whiskey and Gatorade and spent the rest of the day drinking until my limbs felt loose and my head airy. I'd soak myself in oblivion, each glass a cleansing stream melting away the memory of Bingsley's voice and Villers' sneer, of Conner's wide eyes and Taylor's disapproving looks. Of my mother's pleading texts and midnight rants. Filling myself with lightness as the bottle emptied.

Yet all lightness is temporary. I ended up throwing up later that evening, chasing the bile down with a few additional sips of more whiskey that sent me into a fit of violent vomiting until well past midnight on Sunday. It felt like a necessary penance: getting drunk on my own bullshit then purging the poison. The hot liquid rising in my throat with each heave brought me back to my body. Back to my thoughts. Back to the nights when my mother would rant about my father's indiscretions, pinning me down with the weight of her tears. That's probably when I started drinking, finishing up the rest of whatever was in her bottles to see if it offered me the same respite it afforded her. It did, for a while. The Navy offered my only true escape. Being out to sea meant you didn't have to feel guilty about not picking up the phone. Besides, I had to keep working so I could register her as my dependent. None of the part-time jobs my mother landed would cover her heath expenses.

That word—dependent. It sickened me. I heaved another round of metallic-tasting bile into the toilet.

Mom never seemed to escape dependency. Not from my father's money or her Lexapro-and-Pinot cocktails. One brought her status and security. The other brought her release. It also caused her to trip and tumble down the stairs a few years back. She passed out from the pain then dragged herself, inch by excruciating inch, to her phone to call for an ambulance. She gave my name as an emergency contact, but I was deployed at the time and didn't answer. I learned about her accident two days later, when our ship pulled into port and I could check my voicemail. My sister sent me a text about it, saying if I wasn't returning from deployment (my "little vacation," as she called it) to help our mother, she wasn't cutting her time in the Bahamas short either. When I went to our executive officer to request leave to help Mom convalesce, he denied my request.

"Doesn't she have any other family members?" He asked. Before I could answer that no, she didn't, none that were reliable, he added, "If it were your own kids or spouse, then maybe, but I can't approve leave for a parent. That's not how this works. Don't bother escalating this to the captain either, because he'll agree with me. We need you here."

When did all that happen, anyway? Oh. Right. Oman. We went out as a wardroom later that evening and I couldn't seem to stop myself from wanting another drink before I as much as set my lips on the one in my hand. I thought it could dull my fury, keep me from knocking the executive officer off his bar stool, or booking a flight home without approval, or setting my sister's apartment on fire. I wanted to dilute the feeling of being an abject disappointment to the person who needed me the most. Diminish the hatred I felt for myself and everyone around me. The drinks merely refracted these feelings, like a beam of light passing through water.

So much for being dependable, I thought as I rinsed out my mouth and spat into the bowl. Inevitably, I thought of Conner. Someone else I'm bound to fail. The kid was bold, you couldn't deny it. I admired her, the way she could turn her anger outward instead of inward. Maybe I could make the decision I wanted to make. Stand up to Bingsley. Weather Lion's disappointment. But how big a hit would my career take, then? I'm sure integrity is worth something. It sure as shit doesn't pay your mother's medical bills, though.

*

Monday arrived like a punch to the chin. I somehow managed to summon enough strength to shower and proceed to work, albeit without make-up and with my hair in a wet bun, slurping a sports drink between bouts of nausea. I thought—perhaps even hoped—the only way I'd ever leave the bathroom would be if paramedics scraped my desiccated corpse from the tile floor. The possibility of calling in sick crossed my mind, though it would only delay the situation with Villers and Conner. I so badly wanted a drink.

Taylor never returned to the house. Or if he did, I hadn't heard him. When I left for work, his car wasn't in the driveway, his bed hadn't been slept in, and the coffee he brewed most mornings remained unmade. Probably for the best. The thought of drinking anything made me involuntarily gag.

The passageway outside my office bustled with the excitement of a new morning. All midshipmen resided in Bancroft Hall, an enormous dormitory spanning over thirty acres of the campus. Each company occupied the same floor, living and working in proximity to their company officer's office. The intention was to mimic life in a barracks or on a ship, where privacy and personal space failed to exist. The reality was that I had a front-row seat to the bizarre rituals that characterized life at a service academy. Pairs of plebes stood sentry at various posts, preparing to bellow their morning chow calls. Two upperclassmen, clad in their ridiculous black uniform shirts and pants, paced from one pair to the next, murmuring inquiries which were answered with shouted replies. Three guys burst through a set of double doors at the far end of the hall, grass stained and damp-haired, sprinting to their rooms to change in time for formation. The smell of sweat and soil lingered behind them. I scrawled two hasty notes—one to Villers, another to Conner—telling them both to see me in my office at lunch, then passed it to the messenger on watch. The office started spinning. The plebes hollered their incomprehensible warnings that there was ten minutes to morning meal formation. Echoes from other morning chow calls in other passageways resounded down the corridor and stabbed into my brain until I thought it would burst. I dismissed the plebes, refusing to acknowledge their confused looks.

The glare of the morning sun reflecting from the river antagonized me. It felt strangely personal, like the world insisted on my suffering. The sun could fuck itself. I closed the door to the office, shut the blinds, and moved the trash can within reach. If anyone needed me, they'd knock. In the meantime, I stared at the conduct report on my screen and tried to ignore the remaining mini bottle hidden in my bottom desk drawer. I removed it and stroked the smooth plastic. A mere gulp of vodka within my reach, not enough to impair my judgment, just enough to blunt my piecing hangover.

Two hours later, the *Recommendation* field in the conduct report remained blank. I'd added and deleted sentences too many times to count, stopping every ten minutes to caress the bottle in my hand. My body shook with the want of it. The room started to smell like a distillery as I perspired. With an exaggerated moan, I stood, tucked the bottle in the pocket of my uniform, and left my office. I knew what I needed to do.

When I arrived in front of Conner's room, her door was propped open by a black rubber doorstop. I could make out the faint glow of a single desk light reflecting on the waxed linoleum floors. Her room had the impersonal look that most midshipmen rooms possessed: nothing on the floor; a cluttered bookshelf laden with uneven stacks of papers and binders; a few pictures tacked to the cork board on the side of her desk, half hidden by her laptop; a neatly made bed. Nothing adorned the beige walls except a dartboard with a magazine cut-out of Jim Webb tacked to the center bull's-eye. Several darts stabbed through his smiling face.

Conner slumped over her laptop when I entered, looking through the screen more than she looked at it. She jumped slightly when I knocked, then rose sharply from her chair. She looked rigid as she stood, locking her knees so tightly I thought she'd fall forward.

"Thought we weren't meeting you until lunchtime, ma'am," she said. I motioned for her to sit back down.

"We aren't," I said. "I wanted to talk to you first. I've been reading your statement again and something isn't making sense."

"I wrote everything I remember from that day," Conner said.

"Yeah," I replied. "I'm more interested in what's not there. You're not stupid, you know there were plenty of other options. You lost your temper, fine. That's an outburst, maybe a broken glass or two. Tell me why you really did it."

She sighed and looked away from me as she spoke. "I wanted to handle it myself," she said. "I get so tired. Not only of Villers, but of guys like him. I wanted to send a message."

"Would you do it again?" I asked. "Don't bullshit me. Would you?"

"My only regret, ma'am, is that I didn't knock him out entirely."

I didn't answer right away, but walked to her window and surveyed the view. Unlike the view to my office, Conner's room overlooked the Academy grounds. The white stone dorms consumed the landscape, partially obscuring the academic buildings with rounded door frames and corroding brass at the far end of the yard. Uneven brick walkways stretched forward and twisted around each structure. Imposing architecture meant to forge connections with great empires and enduring legacies, all of it named after some important man or another.

"You know, I always had the worst views when I was a mid," I said to Conner without looking at her. "Every room I was assigned faced inward. All I'd see were alleyways or into other people's rooms. I never left my window open because it was too noisy, or it smelled foul from the dumpsters below."

Conner nodded in reply when I turned to face her.

"I'm not going to separate you," I said. "But you have a lot of work ahead. I can't have you getting commissioned and handling weapons one day with anger issues. You'll stand restriction, but you're going to talk to someone down at the Support Center."

"Thank you," Connor said, exhaling her words.

"I also want you to work with a mentor. Lieutenant Taylor Magneson in the Systems Department," I added, looking away from her as I did. "Do you know him? He may be someone who could help."

Conner shook her head and scowled.

"Don't worry," I said. "He's one of the good ones."

"And Villers?" Conner asked.

"I'm not going to separate him either, if that's what you're asking," I said.

"Oh," she replied.

"Look, you're going to be dealing with a lot of Villerses in your life. Sometimes it seems the entire Navy is just one big network of Villers," I said. "Just one long procession of assholes."

"Then why try?" She asked. "Why do this at all?"

"Because you don't have to march along with them," I said. "You can do things differently. And there's so much to gain, too. If you let them chase you away, they're the only ones who benefit."

I directed my gaze out the window again. From this angle, I could see the curling edges of each building. How the solid, immovable stone weathered over the years by the persistence of rain and rising tides.

"Do you think things will ever really get better?" Conner asked softly.

"I don't know," I said, tracing the outline of the mini bottle in my pocket. "I hope so."

And I meant it. More than she'd ever know.

ACKNOWLEDGMENTS

This book, like so many others, started out as a work of individual creativity, realized only by the collective efforts of so many others. I have benefited from the love and guidance of so many teachers, mentors, and friends over the years that it would be impossible to name them all. Please know that any omission is the fault of page limitations, not of gratitude.

To Kristine, Caleb, Gage, Abby, Pedro, David, and the entire Split/Lip team—your passion, dedication, and brilliance astounds me. I am immensely grateful for the opportunity to have worked with all of you.

To the staff, readers, and volunteers at *Proud to Be* and the Southeast Missouri State University Press, *storySouth*, *Line of Advance*, and Middle West Press—thank you for publishing earlier versions of the stories which appear in this collection. Special thanks are in order to Randy Brown, Chris Lyke, and David Ervin for creating enriching forums where military writers can showcase their work. The writing community is better for your stewardship of it. Thank you also to *Military Experience and the Arts*, *The Wrath-Bearing Tree*, and *Minerva Rising* for publishing work which promotes women service members' perspectives.

To Ivelisse Rodriguez—I am indebted to you for your mentorship, instruction, and prescient insight. This collection would never have been published without your guidance. Thank you also to my fellow workshop participants from The Writing Center Short Story Intensive for the editorial and moral support you all provided along the way.

To Matthew Gallagher and Patrick Deer of the Words After War workshop, Kara Krause of the Voices from War workshop, Seema Reza and the entire team at Community Building Art Works, the team at Missouri Humanities and Southeast Missouri State University Press, and faculty and staff at the Fine Arts Work Center—thank you for supporting my work and, more importantly, cultivating communities where veterans can grow as artists. Matt—thank you especially for your leadership in the veteran writing space and the powerful example you provide to all aspiring and established writers.

To Ivelisse Rodriguez, Matthew Gallagher, Liam Corley, Travis Klempan (USNA '06!), Randy Brown, and Katey Schulz for your kind words. Thank you also to Jerri Bell and Tracy Crow, whose book *It's My Country Too: American Military Women's Stories from the American Revolution to Afghanistan* (University of Nebraska Press, 2017) informed the introduction to this collection.

To the English Department faculty and staff at the United States Naval Academy—thank you for the care and dedication you bring with you into the classroom. I am proud to have learned from you all and even prouder to have been able to call you my colleagues. And to the faculty at Red Bank Catholic and Eatontown public schools, whose dedicated educators, coaches, and counselors imbued in me an ongoing love of learning—you have my unending gratitude.

To my family—my parents, Gary and Barbara, for not only encouraging my crazy dreams, but for all the love and encouragement you provided as I sought them out. To my sister, Katelyn, for listening to my earliest stories and reading my slightly more developed ones. And to my in-laws, Jim and Barbara McGhan, who have always been enthusiastic supporters. I love you all.

And finally, to Mike—who knew getting seasick on a YP would lead me to the love of my life? Thank you is insufficient for the million little things you did to help make this book possible. With you, life is always an adventure. I can't wait to see where the next one takes us.

JILLIAN DANBACK-MCGHAN is an author and Navy veteran. Her work appears or is forthcoming in *Military Experience & the Arts, storySouth, Line of Advance, The Wrath-Bearing Tree*, the anthology *Our Best War Stories* (Middle West Press, 2022), and elsewhere. Jillian is the recipient of the 2020 Col. Darron L. Wright Memorial Writing Award and is a graduate of the U.S. Naval Academy, George Mason University, and Georgetown University. She lives in Annapolis, MD with her family.

NOW AVAILABLE FROM SPLIT/LIP PRESS

For more info about the press and titles,
visit us at www.splitlippress.com

Follow us on Instagram and Twitter: @splitlippress